Affairs of State

DOMINIQUE MANOTTI is a professor of nineteenth-century economic history in Paris. She is the author of a number of novels including *Rough Trade* (winner of the French Crime Writers' Association Award), *Dead Horsemeat* and *Lorraine Connection*, all published in English by Arcadia Books. *Dead Horsemeat* was shortlisted for the 2006 Duncan Lawrie International Dagger Award, and *Lorraine Connection* won the same award in 2008.

ROS SCHWARTZ dropped out of university and ran away to Paris in the early seventies. Since 1981 she has translated a wide range of fiction and non-fiction from the French, including novels by Aziz Chouaki, Fatou Diome, Jacqueline Harpman, Sébastien Japrisot, Yasmina Khadra and Dominique Manotti, as well as political scientists Thérèse Delpech and Olivier Roy. She regularly publishes articles and gives workshops and talks on the art of translation. She has recently been made a Chevalier de l'Ordre des Arts et des Lettres in recognition of her translations.

AMANDA HOPKINSON is Professor of Literary Translation and Director of the British Centre for Literary Translation at the University of East Anglia. She is a literary translator from Spanish, French and Portuguese, most recently of *Rage* by the Argentine writer, Sergio Bizzio, and is currently translating the *Notebooks* of José Saramago. She also writes books on Latin American photography, including recent monographs on the Mexican Manuel Álvarez Bravo and the Amerindian Peruvian photographer Martin Chambi.

Affairs of State

DOMINIQUE MANOTTI

Translated from the French by
Ros Schwartz and Amanda Hopkinson

Arcadia Books Ltd
15–16 Nassau Street
London W1W 7AB

www.arcadiabooks.co.uk

First published in the United Kingdom by Arcadia Books 2009
Originally published by Éditions Payot & Rivages as *Nos fantastiques années fric* 2001

ISBN 978-1-906413-49-1

Typeset in Garamond by MacGuru Ltd
Printed and bound in Finland by WS Bookwell

This book is supported by the French Ministry of Foreign Affairs, as part of the Burgess programme run by the Cultural Department of the French Embassy in London.

Liberté • Égalité • Fraternité
RÉPUBLIQUE FRANÇAISE

Arcadia Books supports English PEN, the fellowship of writers who work together to promote literature and its understanding. English PEN upholds writers' freedoms in Britain and around the world, challenging political and cultural limits on free expression. To find out more, visit www.englishpen.org or contact English PEN, 6-8 Amwell Street, London EC1R 1UQ

Arcadia Books distributors are as follows:

in the UK and elsewhere in Europe:
Turnaround Publishers Services
Unit 3, Olympia Trading Estate
Coburg Road
London N22 6TZ

in the US and Canada:
Independent Publishers Group
814 N. Franklin Street
Chicago, IL 60610

in Australia:
Tower Books
PO Box 213
Brookvale, NSW 2100

in New Zealand:
Addenda
PO Box 78224
Grey Lynn
Auckland

in South Africa:
Quartet Sales and Marketing
PO Box 1218
Northcliffe
Johannesburg 2115

Arcadia Books is the *Sunday Times* Small Publisher of the Year

Contents

Prologue / vii
Affairs of State / 1
Afterword / 202
Notes / 206

Money corrupts, money buys, money crushes, money kills, money ruins, money rots men's consciences.

François Mitterrand

Prologue

A mutton stew simmers in a cast-iron pot, filling the air with the aroma of tomato and spices. The kitchen is clean, with a sink, white units, a big fridge and a wooden table in the centre of the room. A hanging light gives out a warm yellow glow. The window is closed against the night and the heat is suffocating. The father, a stocky man with a furrowed face and grey hair, crashes his fist down on the table:

'Not the theatre ... Not my daughter.'

'I'll do as I like.'

His fist strikes her temple and he roars: 'I forbid you ...'

The girl's head lolls backwards, a crack, a red veil in front of her eyes. She reels and clutches at the table. Her mother sobs, wails, pleads and tries to step between them. The two brothers push her into a corner. The younger children have taken refuge in another room, the TV turned up full volume so the neighbours won't hear.

The girl leans forward, resting both hands on the table:

'No one is ever going to forbid me from doing anything, ever again. In two months I'll be eighteen and an adult ...' Tensely, almost spitting: 'An adult, you hear ...'

'An adult ...'

He chokes with rage, grabs a chair and brandishes it as he edges round the table bearing down on her. She feels the heat behind her, turns around, seizes the pot with both hands and throws it at his head. The sauce splashes out in all directions, splattering the walls, the floor and the furniture with streaks of orangey-red fat. She doesn't even feel the burns on her hands, arms and legs, she doesn't hear her mother screaming. Her father raises his hands to his head, sways, slides down and collapses in a heap on the floor amid the chunks of mutton.

The eldest brother rushes over, slaps her, twists her arm behind her back, lifts her, carries her to one of the bedrooms and locks her in. The men are arguing in the kitchen, voices loudly raised. The father doesn't want to call a doctor. A tap's running. Her mother sobs noisily.

They're going to lock me in. They're going to kill me. Her temples are throbbing. She walks over to the window and opens it. The air is cold, the housing estate ill-lit, silent, three storeys down. *Don't think. Get out. Fast, before they come back.* There are two beds in the room. She grabs hold of a mattress, leans over the windowsill, concentrates, aims, lets go. *Quick, the other one, repeat exactly the same movements with accuracy.* It lands on top of the first. A woman's screams in the kitchen. *Quick. Don't think, do it; don't think. Jump.*

She straddles the sill, tensing her muscles like at the gym. She gazes at the mattress, focuses on it with all her energy, takes a deep breath and jumps.

She hits the ground hard and her right ankle cracks. She struggles to her feet. She can stand on it. She runs slowly, limping, into the night, zigzagging between the apartment blocks, avoiding the well-lit areas, listening out. How long for? She stops, her heart in her mouth. She's lost. She sits on some steps, concealed by a dustbin, clasping her knees and her head buried in her arms. Slowly she catches her breath. Her heart's still pounding slightly. Cold, very cold. Her left eye's closed up, there's a sharp pain in her right ankle and the burns on her arms and legs are excruciatingly painful. No ID, no clothes, no money. One thing's for sure: *I'll never go back home.* And another: *They won't come looking for me. As far as they're concerned, I'm dead. Dead.*

June 1985

Outside, it's sunny, summer's around the corner, but the offices of the RGPP, the Paris police intelligence service, are dark and gloomy with their beige walls, grey lino, metallic furniture and tiny north-facing windows overlooking an interior court-yard. In Macquart's office are three comfortable armchairs upholstered in velvet, halogen lamps permanently switched on. A newspaper is spread out on a table, open at page two, the 'Comment' page. Three intelligence service chiefs, men in their fifties wearing dark suits, are leaning over it.

'It's under Guillaume Labbé's byline. Who is this Guillaume Labbé?'

Macquart straightens up.

'In my view, it's Bornand's pseudonym.'

'The President's personal advisor?'

'Who's your source?'

'Simple deduction. Guillaume is the Abbé Dubois's first name ...' A pause. 'Advisor to Philippe Duke of Orleans ...'[1] Silence. 'In any case, Bornand's always felt he has a great deal in common with the statesman portrayed by the historians and memoir-writers of the eighteenth century: intelligent, depraved, a man of influence with connections ... So the pseudonym Guillaume Labbé seems obvious to me. I think he's even used it once before. I must have it on file somewhere.'

'If you say so ...'

They huddle over it and start reading.

In some sectors of the Paris press, one government scandal follows hot on the heels of the last. The wheels of business must be kept oiled.

'If it is him, he's got a nerve. He dictates half the editorials of the satirical weekly the *Bavard Impénitent*, so that's their speciality ...'

After explaining at length how, on the orders of the Defence Minister, the French secret services sank the Rainbow Warrior, *the Greenpeace ship campaigning against French nuclear testing in the Pacific, in a New Zealand port, killing a Portuguese journalist in the process, certain 'investigative' journalists are now kicking up a fuss over the so-called 'Irish of Vincennes' affair, accusing the men from the Élysée special unit ...*

'It's Bornand, for certain. He's the one who set up that unit, who recruited the men working in it, who placed it under the President's direct authority without having to be accountable to anyone. So clearly, it had better succeed. If it goes, he goes.'

'It's definitely Bornand. He loves macho police officers who climb over walls and shoot first, ask questions later.'

'You've got to admit they're more of a turn-on than we are.'

'Order, gentlemen, please.'

... of having planted the weapons themselves in the homes of the Irish terrorists they arrested in August 1982, the day after the fatal bomb attack in rue des Rosiers.[2]

The Rainbow Warrior *affair prompted impartial observers to question the workings of the French Secret Service: mind-boggling incompetence or complex anti-government and anti-Socialist machinations? And what was the source of the leaks that enabled a handful of French journalists to find out more than the New Zealand investigators, and faster? …*

'Shoot down the Foreign Intelligence Service …'

… The Irish affair is even more ambiguous. The 'investigative' journalists who are on the case all receive their tip-offs from the same source: a psychologically unstable individual with a dodgy personality whose testimony has been doing the rounds of the Paris editors for more than a year, without anyone taking him seriously until now. Furthermore, on his own admission – and this is common knowledge – he is in the pay of one of our major police departments working on the Secret Service's patch.'

'Well, well …'
'An attack on the Directorate for Territorial Surveillance too … For the time being, the intelligence services seem to have emerged remarkably unscathed.'
'He's not on top form today.'

Have these 'investigative' journalists questioned this informer's reliability? Have they tried to cross-check the information he has given them with other sources? Not at all.

The aim is clear: to discredit the Élysée unit, the team of police officers and gendarmes responsible for protecting the President's security and coordinating the fight against terrorists in France. A crack team which has been successful in every case it has handled and which has, let it be said loud and clear, dealt a serious blow to the spread of terrorism in France with the arrest of the Irish in August '82.

The three men straighten up in unison.

'I bet he believes it.'

'Impressive.'

This unit continues to centralise and store all intelligence on terrorism, seeking to coordinate the numerous police and gendarmerie departments concerned and plays a key part in international counter-terrorism cooperation. In short, its role is eminently positive and paves the way for setting up a national security council on the model of the American NSC. Its remit will be to support the President and provide him with analyses and briefings on national security issues.

'It's Bornand, without a doubt. Staunchly pro-American since his teens.'

'We underestimated him. The man's a poet.'

So who gains from discrediting this crucial mechanism? The traditional police departments which feel threatened, those whose incompetence, inefficiency, infighting and self-defeating rivalry are blatant, and whose chiefs are afraid of losing their powers and their privileges and who, need we be reminded, have never been excessively fond of President Mitterrand.

Guillaume Labbé.

'What do you think?' asks Macquart.

'What's bitten him? If it is him. It's less than a year until the election and all the polls, including ours, indicate that the Socialists will lose. This isn't exactly the best time to start a war between the President's private police force and the official police department.'

'The war's already on. Against the Élysée unit. The press campaign on the Irish of Vincennes hasn't come out of the blue. I think that Bornand's simply mistaken his target, it's his old animosity towards the official police resurfacing.'

'Is this a storm in a teacup or is it dangerous?'

'Bornand, if it is him, is a personal friend of President Mitterrand. Definitely influential, but a lone sniper who's becoming increasingly isolated.'

'So, much ado about nothing ...'

'You can't be too careful. I'll take another look at his file.'

♣

All morning Noria has been logging reports of lost and stolen cars, mopeds, handbags, dogs, household tools, wines lovingly laid down in a cellar (with the list of châteaux, watch the spelling, the plaintiff is a connoisseur). She's now been a police officer based in the 19th *arrondissement* of Paris for two months, after more than a year of hardship, poverty, hostels, casual jobs on the side. Far from the dense tangle of family hatred and violence. Far too from her school friends, the occasional caring teacher, books devoured in secret, and from the school drama society. Getting up on stage, existing in her own right while playing the part of another, had been an illuminating discovery. It all now seemed a long way away, all that, a world out of reach ... Now her one obsession was to find a way of earning her living. Fast.

Having reached the age of eighteen, there were the formalities for getting duplicates of her ID, assisted by women's organisations, and the endless hanging around at various town halls, where by chance an ad had caught her eye: 'Recruitment competition. Police officers. Baccalaureate required.'

Baccalaureate. She'd had to leave school at sixteen to help her mother, and anyway, studying wasn't for girls. Not for boys either for that matter. Her two older brothers had better things to do around the neighbourhood. Baccalaureate. *I haven't got it either, but I'm bright enough. A police officer. A steady job. Better than that, an ID card, a place in the world, a role to play, on the side of the law, on the side of power.*

And today, like every other day, forms in triplicate, including one for the insurance company, the usual routine. The routine, this morning, is the secret and mysterious disappearance of 174 clandestinely lacquered ducks from kitchens in lower Belleville apartments, destined for the Chinese restaurants that have sprung up there. Gang warfare, blackmail, a racket, a raid by the hungry? No one at the precinct feels exactly at home in the local Chinatown. And now a distraction: the superintendent calls Noria into his office.

'Be an angel and take this file,' (beige cardboard cover, containing photocopies). 'Fifteen or so complaints about the same problem, in the same place, in less than a month. It's not a case of major importance, but it is causing quite a lot of bad feeling. I had a call from the deputy mayor, the elections are getting close. Go and interview the plaintiffs. Reassure these good women, show them that the police takes citizens' concerns seriously and are on the case. I'm counting on you. I want a report this evening.'

'Very good, Superintendent.'

Be an angel. Would it kill him to say my name, Noria Ghozali? She feels choked. Fearing the worst, she picks up the file and sits down in a vacant office to read it.

Four women aged between sixty-seven and eighty-five, all living in one of the reputedly peaceful 'villages' in the 19th *arrondissement*, on top of a hill. The grannies state that they're terrified to leave their homes, because, for about a month, fire-crackers hidden in dog mess explode as they walk past, splattering them with dog shit.

Noria takes a deep breath. The youngest, the only woman, the only cop of North African origin, a mere officer, a lowly, precarious status. *Naturally, I get to deal with the dog shit. Maybe when I 'grow up', I'll be given the dogs that get run over. Huh, some promotion.*

A list of the four 'victims' and their addresses, all up on Buttes Chaumont. She walks up the hill. Quiet, narrow streets, not many cars, a few passers-by who stop to greet each other and pause for a chat, brick houses built close together offering a panoramic view of Montmartre as a bonus. On this sunny day, the Sacré Cœur gleams white, looking like a mosque with its minaret-like bell tower.

First on the list, Madame Aurillac, seventy-five years old, owner of a little restaurant serving a dish of the day for more than four decades. Five complaints from her alone. A low house, restaurant on the ground floor, and on the first floor, two vast windows hung with white brocade curtains. Noria pushes open the door. Four elderly women are sitting at one of the tables, gossiping and laughing. There's a half-empty bottle of Suze – only eleven o'clock in the morning and they're already sozzled.

'Madame Aurillac?' inquires Noria.

The four women stare at her, sizing her up. Average height, shapeless in brown cotton trousers and jacket, a round, slightly moon-shaped face, olive skin, big, impenetrable black eyes beneath heavily drawn eyebrows, and black hair scraped back in a tight bun.

'Too severe and a terrible hairdo,' says the first woman.

A bleached blonde caked with make-up inquires: 'Are you new?'

'Perhaps we could emphasise her exotic side,' says the third.

Noria flashes her ID: 'Police.'

Consternation among the old girls. A woman with dyed hair and a frizzy perm gets up, a black apron around her waist, and slippers on her feet:

'I'm Madame Aurillac. It's a mistake. We had an appointment with an applicant …'

'For a job as a cleaner,' adds the blonde.

So they did. The applicant arrives, hair immaculately styled, make-up, high heels, short black skirt and pink cotton vest revealing her navel, breasts spilling out, larger than life. Madame Aurillac rushes over to her, drags her into the street, has a few words with her and comes back into the restaurant alone.

'This is a reputable establishment, you know. Ask Inspector Santoni, he often eats here.'

Santoni, macho, fat belly and apparently well connected in the neighbourhood. That's all she needs.

'Would you like a drink, a little Suze maybe?'

'No, thank you. I've come to see you regarding your complaints about the firecrackers …'

'We lodged a complaint too,' chorus the others.

'It's not just the firecrackers. Ill-bred little hooligans, they come from the housing estates down below and cause havoc up here.'

'They play football in the street late at night, with their radios turned up full blast, playing that jungle music.'

'Would you be able to recognise them?'

'They're all the same, these Arabs ...' Madame Aurillac trails off in mid-sentence, gazing at Noria, bemused. 'That's not what I meant ...'

'I don't quite understand what you did mean.'

'Do you think you can stop these goings-on?'

'I'll keep you posted.'

She rises.

'Are you sure, not even a little drop?'

Outside, she takes a deep breath to steady herself. A report by this evening ... On what? The gang of pimping grannies? Santoni's leisure activities? *Frankly I'd have preferred the disappearing lacquered ducks.*

I'll go and check out the housing estate down there. Just opposite is a shop selling toys, games, stationery and books, run by a hunched, smiling elderly couple wearing white dust jackets.

'Police,' says Noria. They exchange looks, the woman slips behind the man. 'Routine enquiry. Do you sell firecrackers?'

'Of course. Especially at this time of year with it being nearly the 14th of July. Like all toy shops. Isn't that right, missus?' he says, turning to his wife.

She nods.

'Firecrackers with a slow-burning fuse?'

'Those too, yes.'

He hesitates. He knows about the exploding dog shit, obviously. But as for calling the police ...

'And your customers are ...'

'Here they come,' says the little old woman. 'As always when it's a sunny lunchtime.'

Two kids, aged ten to twelve, wearing jogging suits, arrogant little machos. Noria takes them by the hand and leads them over to a bench, opposite the shop.

'Noria Ghozali, police officer.'

'Nasser,' says the taller of the two.

The introductions are now over.

'The firecrackers in the dog shit up on the hill, is that you?'

'What's the problem? We're not the first, and we're not the only ones ...'

'But you're the last. You stop, you tell your friends to stop, we'll forget all about it. I'm sure you'll find something else. You have to be flexible.'

Back to HQ. Noria crosses the duty room, greeting the uniformed officers, starts going up the stairs to the offices on the first floor and stops. Pinned to the wall are three little photocopied posters: 'No Arab scum in the French police', and a target on a shape that resembles her. She stands rooted to the step. Alone. *Don't give in. It's not about you.* She makes her way slowly to the toilet, her body rigid, and locks herself in. She washes her hands thoroughly, then her face, staring at herself in the mirror and straightens her bun. Then she goes back to her office and writes her report. Authors of the attacks identified. Problem sorted.

At the end of the day, she goes back down the stairs, her stomach in a knot. The posters are gone. She crosses the duty room, walking past the uniformed officers in silence.

Thursday 28 November

A plane leaves a trail in an intense blue sky very high above a range of bare, snow-covered mountains and an opaque green lake. A standard ad for a budget airline company. And then the plane bursts into flames, explodes, and breaks up into a dozen huge fireballs shooting out stars before spinning down towards the earth amid a shower of burning debris. The noise of the explosion reverberates in the mountains, echoing endlessly.

A comfortable sitting room in shades of beige and chestnut: two leather sofas, a few deep armchairs, a glass and steel coffee table, thick white wool carpeting, two large windows blocked out by heavy velvet curtains. On the wall, a mildly saucy earth-red chalk drawing by Boucher, lit by a spotlight, depicts a plump young nude being gracefully humped by a young man whose clothing is barely loosened. Men aged between forty and sixty, in deeply conventional dark suits and ties, chat and drink champagne, whisky and cocktails served by women aged between twenty and thirty moving from one to the other, smiling and attentive. They all look superb in their revealing, beautifully cut, figure-hugging dresses in dark colours with discreetly plunging necklines and tasteful jewellery, smiling all the time.

The men have just closed a deal to sell arms to Iran, a thousand missiles. The sale is illegal, since the country is under an embargo, so naturally tensions are running high. Especially since the delivery date had had to be postponed for a few days at the last minute. Luga Airport in Malta, through which the cargo was to transit, had just been the scene of a pitched battle between Egypt's special forces and a group of Palestinians who had taken the passengers and crew of an Egyptian aircraft hostage. Several dozen dead later, the airport was finally cleared, flights resumed yesterday, and this morning, the Boeing 747 cargo laden with missiles took off from Brussels-Zavantem heading for Tehran, via Valetta, Malta. It should already have landed in Tehran. And now, the deal done, it's time to celebrate.

Bornand plays the host. Tall, very slim, an attractive sixty-year-old with thick, wavy hair, more pepper than salt, and a long face whose features are emphasised by a network of vertical furrows and a thick, neatly trimmed, completely white moustache. His light grey tailored suit, cut to a neat fit, emphasises his slimness as he moves from group to group saying a few words, touching a shoulder, filling a glass.

Flandin, the boss of the SEA,[3] the applied electronics company which sold the missiles to the Iranians, his left hand on a girl's buttocks, holding a glass of champagne in his right, is in conversation with a tall, fat Lebanese banker who's giving an animated description of a camel race in the desert, organised by a Saudi prince. Flandin laughs, and when Bornand comes over, he raises his glass:

'To our host, gentlemen, who pulled out all the stops to ensure the success of this deal.'

Bornand responds to the toast. *Flandin. I picked the right man. An excellent electronics engineer, but a somewhat limited company boss, always short of capital, and chasing business. The perfect supplier, still under our control. And now, he's here, thrilled*

to be hobnobbing with the rich and powerful, with the added
excitement of being part of an illegal operation at no risk to himself.

'And to all the deals to come,' adds the Lebanese banker.

'We'd better believe it,' answers Bornand, smiling.

Karim, a friend for over a decade, with whom he went into partnership to found the IBL, International Bank of Lebanon,[4] a key broker in all Middle Eastern arms deals, of which there are many.

The banker leans over to the girl being groped by Flandin, pops a breast out of her dress and slowly trickles champagne over her curvaceous quivering flesh until it runs down to her nipple, when he then drinks it avidly.

Bornand pours himself a glass of champagne. *Restore the balance of French policy in the Middle East, resume relations with Iran. This is where realpolitik is decided, in the drawing room of a brothel, and I am the chief architect.*

An Iranian officer, sprawled in an armchair, his eyes half closed, a blissful look on his face, is smoking a cigarette which Katryn has just rolled for him, to which she has added a pinch of heroin. Katryn, a real slave. She is sitting on the arm of the chair. A helmet of black hair, pallid complexion, red lips. She leans towards him; he follows her with his gaze, fascinated, an iridescent pearl, hanging from an invisible thread around her neck, quivering in the hollow of her throat at her every movement, bobbing when she speaks, a pearly counterpoint to the whiteness of her face. She listens attentively and knowingly. The officer, wallowing in nostalgia, tells her of the past splendours of the Shah's court, snipe-hunting in the terraced paddy fields on the slopes of Mount Elbrus, and the descent through the orange groves to the shores of the Caspian Sea. Bornand mentally flashes back, picturing the snipes' lively, erratic flight against a sky of the deepest blue. She prompts him when he tails off, as if she had been a part of these excursions since childhood: hard work this, keeping him talking rather than fucking.

Bornand leans towards her, takes her hand, brushes it with his lips, his moustache tickles, and walks off.

A discreet buzzing, the intercom. Bornand goes behind the bar in the corner of the room, and picks up the receiver.

'François, a phone call for you. I took the risk of disturbing you, it sounds very urgent.'

'Coming.'

In the lobby, Mado, the mistress of the house, is waiting for him and points to a booth. He picks up the phone.

'François? Pontault here. I hope you're enjoying your little party …'

'You're not calling me just to say that?'

'… because it's not going to last long. Turkey has just announced that a Boeing 747 cargo plane has vanished from its airspace …'

Bornand convulsively clenches the glass he's holding in his left hand. It smashes, cutting through to the bone at the base of his thumb. Shards of glass, blood on his hand, his shirt, his trousers, the carpet, the walls of the phone booth.

'… Above Lake Van to be exact, coming in from Malta …'

Bornand frantically tries to staunch the bleeding with his shirt tails.

'We don't know what happened yet, but there's no doubt it's our plane. François, are you there? Now what do we do?'

The bleeding is more or less under control.

'Like all true gamblers, we double the stakes. I'll call you tomorrow morning.'

Friday 29 November

The telephone rings, early on this particular morning. Bornand surfaces slowly from a heavily drugged sleep and gropes around. A shooting pain in his left hand, a brutal reminder of the evening at Mado's, the vanished plane, blood spurting everywhere. He picks up the telephone blindly.

'Morning, François. André Bestégui here. Am I waking you up?'

A long sigh:

'How did you guess? What do you want at this hour?'

'To see you. Very soon, and to talk.'

'About what? At least give me a clue.'

'About the plane that disappeared yesterday over Turkey.'

'Later, over lunch, one o'clock at the Carré des Feuillants?'

'Perfect.'

He replaces the receiver. Bestégui. Bornand had first come across him way back in 1960, during the Algerian War of Independence, at the offices of his import-export company, avenue de la Grande-Armée. He'd been a slightly self-conscious young student in a modern décor of electric blue carpeting and steel furniture, with a painting by Nicolas de Staël on a white wall. There was a stunning receptionist who had no objections to working overtime entertaining important clients. Easy to dazzle, easy to seduce. Bornand had no hesitation in doing both, just in case, and he'd been right to cultivate Bestégui. Nowadays, Bestégui represents the type of French investigative journalism that Bornand most abhors, but it's always useful to have friends in the right places. Look after Bestégui.

He is awake now, contemplating the orange, red and brown bedspread. Things are looking clearer. Not an accident, an attack. A sudden attack. The plane disappeared yesterday, the press hears about it the same day. In a way, good. He's going to have to be very effective. Aim: find out who, exactly, was behind the strike.

It's going to be a busy day. He's up. In the burgundy and white tiled bathroom, he takes a freezing cold shower, as is customary on important days and grooms himself meticulously with a series of rapid, efficient movements. He has no particular liking for his long, skinny body with protruding rounded shoulders and skin that sags in places. Nor for his heavy, bony face and too pale blue eyes. But he's as obsessive about his appearance as a professional lothario. He shaves, carefully trims his moustache, splashes on aftershave, styles his hair with gel and applies cologne before getting dressed. It's the season for closely tailored cashmere and silk suits in every shade of grey. And today he selects a red and grey Hermès tie.

The day begins, as always, with his morning stroll with the President.

It's a dull day with icy rain falling in huge heavy drops, at times it feels like sleet. They walk through the streets side by side, two silhouettes in woollen coats, scarves and felt hats, heading towards the Élysée. Bornand, in his long, tailored coat and pearl-grey fedora, looks like a 1920s dandy. He leans slightly towards the President, who is stockier. The two old friends chat idly of this and that.

Earlier their paths had crossed several times, one a lawyer, the other his client. No more. Then came 1958 and De Gaulle's accession to power, and Mitterrand emerged among the French political elite as one of the few opponents of the General who wasn't a member of the Communist Party. Long conversations between him and Bornand. They found they shared a faith in the Atlantic Alliance, and the same visceral anti-Gaullism, the same anti-Communism mediated by their understanding of the Party. Going further still, they touched on possible shared sympathies during the war, without probing deeper. Bornand developed a profound admiration for Mitterrand's subtlety and skilful political manoeuvring. He found himself on the fringes of the political power machine, excluded from political circles, ostracised in a way since the end of the war. Condemned to low-level pro-American conspiracies and wheeling and dealing that was lucrative but gave him no status, Bornand saw this budding friendship as his chance to enter the worthy sphere of French politics at last. He offered Mitterrand his services, and that was the beginning of a lasting association during which Bornand played a shadowy role in the President's entourage, which suits him perfectly, until he became his advisor at the Élysée in 1981, and one of Mitterrand's chosen companions on his Parisian walks.

'The latest news from Gabon … President Omar Bongo has put on weight recently …'

A hint of anxiety in the deep voice. The President is joking already. Bornand takes his time.

'… I heard it from Akihito, his regular tailor. Ten centimetres around the waist in two months.' A pause. 'At the Franco-African summit in La Baule, he'll be wearing long, double-breasted jackets.'

'In that case, if I were him, I'd change tailor.'

'So would I. But Akihito has other qualities. He sent five gorgeous blondes to deliver the suits. Whom he had a bit of trouble recruiting, incidentally.'

'I don't believe it …'

'There are rumours about Bongo's health …'

The President and Bornand stop in front of a luxury couturier's window. Two young sales assistants observe them from inside the shop, and smile. The President waves at them before resuming his walk.

'The little brunette's a stunner.'

Bornand takes note, then takes the plunge:

'A plane crashed yesterday in Turkey …' The President gives him a sidelong glance. 'There's a rumour in the Parisian press that the plane was carrying French arms to Iran.'

'Don't tell me you're going to start talking to me about arms deals too, it seems to be all the rage at the moment … and to Iran what's more! A country under international embargo … If people are stupid enough to go in for that kind of deal, let them pay the price.' A few steps in silence. 'You know very well that I'm very much against selling arms to warmongering countries as a matter of principle.'

'It's a rule that can be bent a little when it comes to Iraq. Only two days ago the *Tehran Times* accused us of having delivered to Iraq five Super-Étendard fighters, twenty-four Mirage F1s, and the ultra-modern missiles that are destroying Iranian oil installations. And they weren't wrong …'

The President quickens his pace.

'Don't spoil this beautiful walk in the rain. I don't want to hear any more talk of arms sales to Iraq.' He turns to Bornand. 'And you know it. Talk to the ministers concerned.'

They walk on in silence for a moment.

'I'm not talking to you about arms sales, but about France's role in the Middle East ...'

'France is not Iran's enemy ...'

'That won't be sufficient.'

'... but in the Middle East, the age-old balance between Arabs and Persians must be maintained.'

A gesture of irritation:

'Let's look at this another way. Instead of talking about arms, let's talk about elections. We have four French hostages who've been held in Lebanon for between seven and nine months. The ministers concerned, to use your expression, are playing the Syria card, and after all this time they haven't even managed – I won't even say to enter into negotiations with the hostage-takers – but simply to find out who they are and what they want. I can tell you the key to the hostage affair lies in Tehran, as everyone knows, and I am capable of securing their release.'

'The hostages' release is one of the government's ongoing preoccupations, and it is continually working towards a solution, which I approve of.' A silence. Then the President adds: 'Of course, anything you can do to assist in Tehran will be welcome, as I've already told you.'

'But unofficially. Officially, we have broken off relations with Iran. At least give my contacts a clear signal. Otherwise, there'll be no progress on the hostages before the general election, and March '86 is just around the corner.'

After a few more paces in silence, the President embarks on a monologue on Saint-John Perse. Bornand switches off and massages the palm of his left hand. Shooting pains. How to find out who ordered the disappearance of the plane?

The President stops, his face waxen, leaning for a moment on Bornand's arm.

'All things considered, it is certain that it would be better for the Parisian press to talk about your contacts with Iran rather than this unfortunate plane crash.'

This was the green light he'd been waiting for.

Bornand drops into the Élysée unit headquarters and finds only two young women at their desks. The previous day's telephone taps have been transcribed, and they'll be sorted and classified before being passed on, as every day, to the President's secretariat. Bornand sits down for a moment and accepts a coffee, with two sugars, asks how their children are and complains about the miserable weather. There's snow on the way. He flicks through the files rapidly. It's one of life's small pleasures that Bornand regularly enjoys: lifting the lid of the hive and watching the bees make honey. But today he knows what he's looking for and he hasn't got time to hang around: he's after all yesterday's calls involving Bestégui, code name: the Basque. At least ten made to the newspaper's office. Various appointments. Interesting, one with the General Secretary of the Paris Mayor's office. Well, well. Covering his rear with a view to the upcoming elections? His daughter has an ear infection. Restoux won't file his article in time, it will have to be held over until the following week. A furious tantrum ensues. Bestégui's writing a substitute under a new pseudonym (Rancourt, make a note, just in case). And lastly, someone called Chardon announces he has a dynamite dossier on a plane crammed with French missiles heading for Iran, which vanished in mid-flight yesterday over Turkey. The Basque warily advises him to be more discreet on the telephone and agrees to meet him that evening at seven p.m.

That was it.

Bornand crosses the street and climbs the steps of the Élysée. His office is a comfortable little room under the eaves, with two windows looking out over the rooftops. Plenty of calm and light. Huge mahogany cupboards lining two walls, kept permanently locked, good armchairs, a few nineteenth-century English engravings depicting hunting scenes with hounds, green carpet and curtains. And in the centre of the room, an English pedestal desk, with a tan leather top. Sitting on it are a notepad, a crystal tumbler filled with pens and felt-tips, and a coloured glass art deco lamp.

Fernandez is waiting for him. A cop Bornand first met ten years ago on the racecourses, when he was working in Intelligence for the Racing and Gambling division. Very young, fairly tall, broad shoulders and flat stomach; short, dark hair, swarthy complexion, a somewhat loud taste in clothes, flashy gold bracelet watch and a signet ring on his middle left finger, tight trousers and colourful shirts. Good-looking guy, in a way, and very keen on easy, good-looking girls: sharing women had soon created a bond between them. Intelligent: it didn't take him long to understand how to network in racing circles, and who the guys with real power are. Enterprising: always looking to make a deal, or a financially useful social contact. And left-wing, in other words, he liked Bornand and trusted him when he was still a long way from power. So when Bornand arrived at the Élysée, he had him transferred from Intelligence to his personal security, which opened up new career prospects for Fernandez and confirmed he had made the right political choices. A bit too much of a lout to be truly integrated into the inner family circle, but a distant cousin for whom Bornand feels a certain fondness.

'I've got a job for you, my friend.'

Bornand opens the notebook, selects a green felt-tip and begins to draw complicated squiggles with application, his long, slender hands never still. A silence, before he continues:

'A journalist has approached Bestégui offering to sell him some strictly confidential information about our contacts with Iran and our dealings to secure the hostages' release, which include arms deliveries. We've already talked about this, haven't we?' Fernandez nods. 'Have you heard of a guy called Chardon?'

'Never.'

Bornand slowly jots down a few words, looking distracted, then looks up.

'Bestégui seems to know him though. If this makes the headlines, the Iranians will break off talks. We have to identify the people behind this Chardon guy and shut them up. And to do that, I'm relying on you. If he's mixed up in this sort of business, Intelligence must have him on file. You're going to ask them for me. Then, depending on what they come up with, you're going to find this Chardon, try and glean anything that might shed light on what's in his dossier and who his sources are. You can call me here, or at the Carré des Feuillants at lunchtime.' He rubs the palm of his left hand which is still giving him shooting pains. 'Be smart, Fernandez. We need results.'

Once Fernandez has left, Bornand sets to work.

The first thing is to find suppliers with stocks of missiles available, preferably overseas. *I'll check out Meister in Hamburg. If news of the scandal breaks after the arrival of a new delivery to Tehran, we'll come out of it relatively unscathed.* Then, make amends where possible. And don't expect any help from government departments on that front, turn to the family first. A basic rule of self-preservation. First of all, Pontault, one of the Defence minister's staff. A gendarme. A friend of some of the men in the unit. His father, also a gendarme, ended his career as head of security at Bornand's father-in-law's firm. He's loyal. He takes it upon himself to remind all concerned that the missiles sent to Iran had been purchased from the French army, following all the correct procedures. Clearly the military wouldn't like their financial transactions and methods to become public knowledge. Nor would the politicians at the Ministry, who took their cut from the deal. So, defence secrets all the way down the line. Pontault acts as guarantor. Covered on that front. Bornand notes the date, time and content of the telephone call.

Distraction: an appointment with an Israeli agent he met in Washington and who's passing through Paris on his way back from a trip to Côte-d'Ivoire. Not long to go before the Franco-African summit opens. Exchange of information. The Côte-d'Ivoire recognises the State of Israel and is playing a growing role in arms smuggling to South Africa. A link between the two? In any case, large quantities of arms are currently circulating in the region. Always good to know in case Hamburg doesn't respond.

Bornand writes a summary of the conversation for the President, expurgated of all reference to arms deals, since he doesn't want to know.

It's time to meet Bestégui at the restaurant. On the way, a detour via the couturier's window where the President paused this morning. He buys a vicuña scarf and asks the pretty brunette sales assistant to take it to the Élysée that afternoon. The President will appreciate it.

♣

Extract from Chardon's intelligence service record:

> Chardon, Jean-Claude. Born 1953, in Vincennes, Val-de-
> Marne, where his father ran a hardware shop. Baccalaureate
> in literature, 1973. Then joined the marine infantry, served for
> five years in Gabon and Côte-d'Ivoire. Returned in 1978 as a
> lieutenant. In 1980, he was tried and convicted for living off
> immoral earnings. He then reinvented himself as a journalist,
> freelancing for *France-Dimanche* and *Ici Paris* under various
> pseudonyms (the most frequent: Franck Alastair, Teddy
> Boual, Jean Georges) mainly writing gossip columns about
> the private lives of showbiz celebrities and the jet set.
> Numerous known liaisons with call girls and models who
> act as informers. Since the immoral earnings case in 1980,
> no further complaints have been lodged against him. He
> currently resides at 38 rue Philippe-Hecht, Paris 19, in a house
> which he owns.

A rather brief record. It is highly likely that he must be
earning a bit on the side from blackmail. But what the hell's he
doing mixed up in an arms deal? At least it's a starting point.

Fernandez starts tailing Chardon when he leaves home at 11.47
a.m. Brown corduroy trousers, heavy work boots, khaki parka,
unremarkable features and shaggy, lifeless chestnut hair. Fernandez feels good-looking in comparison. Some fifty metres
further on, Chardon turns into avenue Mathurin-Moreau,
walks down to the metro at Colonel-Fabien, and goes into
the Brasserie des Sports, Fernandez hard on his heels. It is

a busy bar adjacent to a large restaurant with around forty tables, separated by curtains of green foliage, a buzz of voices, mainly regulars, but at this hour, still plenty of free tables. A waiter recognises Chardon and signals to him that someone is waiting for him at the back of the room. Fernandez follows him from a distance, then pauses and takes cover behind a line of bamboos. Chardon clearly knows the girl who's waiting for him. It's Katryn, a call girl whom Bornand regularly uses. *Be prudent.* Concealed by the plants, Fernandez manages to sit not far from them. They order two beef and carrot casseroles, and half a bottle of Côtes. Fernandez watches. They start a relaxed conversation about this and that. Coffee, bill, they go Dutch. Then they wander over for a chat with the woman owner at the till and go down to the basement via a staircase right next to the bar. After a few minutes Fernandez attempts to follow them. But the owner stops him: the toilets and telephone are at the back of the restaurant to the left. Downstairs there's only a snooker table, and someone's using it. Fernandez curses. That has to be where important matters are under discussion. He calls Bornand.

'Katryn. Holy shit.' *Last night, with the Iranian. Familiarity … Perhaps they already know each other?* She lays on the hero number, wheedles information out of him, she's capable of it. It reaches Chardon … Possibly. But who are the pair of them working for? *It's a lead, Fernandez, don't lose them.*

Fernandez props himself up at the bar and orders a coffee and brandy.

In the basement is a narrow, windowless room with a snooker table in the centre. A suspended copper lamp shines a glaring light on the green baize, plunging everything around into darkness. Chardon sets up the balls in the triangle and removes the frame. He plays first, his head and torso in the circle of light. Too fast, too hard. The triangle shatters, a series of dry clacks, no score. He straightens up, steps back into the shadows and asks:

'Have you got anything new for me?'

Katryn appears not to hear him. She stalks round the snooker table in her tight black jeans and black polo-neck sweater, her piercing eyes concentrating on the baize. Then she leans over, her black hair reflecting the light, the cue slides smoothly, one precise move and ball number four plops into a corner pocket. She plays again, too quickly, misses. She sighs and straightens up.

'There was a piece of news, three weeks ago.'

'You already told me.'

'Are you playing?'

He plays almost randomly. Nothing.

Katryn begins a kind of dance around the baize. She moves slowly, leans half her body into the light, straightens up, starts walking again. Then makes up her mind, and lines up three shots in a row, talking all the while.

'Three days ago, Lentin and his buddies came to train her.'

'Lentin, the film producer?'

'That's him. He's used to this type of operation at Mado's.'

She leans forward, in silence. Then he continues:

'Mado thinks that to be a true professional, you need experience. And she's right about that. She tends to keep the training period down to a minimum in the interests of profitability.'

Chardon plays again, without success. Katryn, irritated, lightly taps the light shade with her cue, and the table oscillates between light and darkness.

'You're not concentrating hard enough, this is no game.'

'So what about Lentin?'

'This time, the training session degenerated. Lentin had come with two of his friends, novices at this game. I have no idea what happened, perhaps the girl had a romantic idea of the job, or she'd been conned into it from the start. Anyway, she ended up with a broken nose, a couple of broken ribs and her back slashed. Mado had a real job calming her down. She sent her back home to Périgueux.' She slides a piece of paper folded into four onto the baize. 'Her name and address. You can get her to tell you her story. I know, it's risky. But she's not even fifteen. Lentin will pay up to keep her quiet. And now, how about giving me a proper game of snooker?'

♣

Bestégui is waiting for Bornand at the Carré des Feuillants. As always, Bornand's running late. A hushed atmosphere. He slowly sips a pure malt whisky and relaxes. Their paths first crossed in 1960, when he wasn't even twenty, during the Algerian War of Independence. A luxurious, uncluttered office. Him feeling lost, adrift, vulnerable. Bornand had the reputation of being a diabolical boss, a staunch supporter of decolonisation since the days of the Indochina war and with ongoing business relations with the Provisional Government of the Algerian Republic,[5] and there were even rumours of arms sales to the National Liberation Front. There was something of the buccaneer about him, and he was elegant and well-spoken, with a penchant for irony. Yes, he was willing to support the French national student union's demonstrations of solidarity with the Algerian students.

'It's high time you took some public initiatives. This war is bleeding our economy and boosting de Gaulle,' Bornand had said.

He had signed a cheque in support, and gone on the student demonstration in October 1960 with a few of his friends, including François Mitterrand, who received a few blows from the cops' batons witnessed by journalists. That's not something you forget when you're twenty.

Bestégui is still elegant, rich, self-confident and highly informed. Incidentally, how many articles has he penned, including some that have helped build Bornand's reputation among Paris's elite? A vast number ... and a few dirty tricks too. You don't get anything for nothing.

Bornand arrives at last and, without apologising, squeezes Bestégui's arm warmly by way of a vague embrace, like a man in a hurry, then sits down. The head waiter hastens over. Bornand doesn't open the menu.

'I'll have what you're having. I trust your judgement.'

Bestégui orders a cream of chestnut soup and pheasant. Bornand eats without even noticing what's on his plate. He has always considered a taste for fine cuisine as incongruous. He only frequents good or very good restaurants because in France they are the undeniable external trappings of wealth, as well as reliable indicators of the esteem in which one holds one's guest. He is fully engrossed in what Bestégui is telling him.

'I've been offered a dossier on a plane that crashed in Turkey yesterday morning. It was supposedly carrying French missiles destined for Iran.' Bornand doesn't bat an eyelid. 'I'd like to know what I might be getting myself into before going any further.'

Apparently he's playing fair, which will make things easier.

'You can hardly expect me to tell you that.'

Bestégui continues, ignoring Bornand's reply: 'In your view, is a deal like that possible, or probable, or am I likely to find myself walking into a trap?'

'That's certainly a possibility. Even a probability. Nearly all the world's arms dealers are doing business with Iran. Embargos have never prevented arms from being sold, they just make them more expensive, and the profits are higher.' He leans towards Bestégui, who is tucking into his food. 'Which doesn't necessarily rule out the possibility that it could be a sting.'

'I'm listening.'

'Allow me to make a little detour via Lebanon where the French hostages are being held. Yesterday I was with a Lebanese friend who was telling me about the outbreak of the current war between the militias, one of the most violent that Beirut has seen – and Beirut has seen many such conflicts. An Amal militiaman, a Muslim and an ally of the Syrians, was driving at breakneck speed as usual, and at a crossroads he demolished the car of a Progressive Socialist Party militiaman, an ally of the Syrians and of Amal. Out came the guns, and war was declared between Amal and the PSP. There are countless French envoys supposedly negotiating the hostages' release in Lebanon. Our lot are wandering around carrying suitcases stuffed with money and speaking on behalf of some minister or other, or the President, or a political party or whatever. You can just imagine. Lebanon's in a state of chaos, about which they're utterly clueless. The result: nothing. Nothing. André, even after more than six months, and for one very simple reason: the key to the hostages isn't in Lebanon, it's in Tehran. And that plane may be part of a much bigger deal.'

'Can you tell me any more about this hypothetical deal?'

'Point number one: it could be a question of stopping arms deliveries to Iraq, or of balancing deliveries to both sides, which the cargo in question may or may not be a part of.'

'If the plane is part of this deal, there are some people who have an interest in preventing it from reaching Tehran.'

'You're telling me.'

'Can you be more specific?'

'Not yet. But if we look at the people who want us to lose the election in March '86, we should come up with the answer. And track them down. Fast.'

Bestégui attacks his chocolate and pistachio dessert.

'Will I get to hear of it first?'

'You won't publish anything about the plane for the moment? And you'll put off the competition?'

'The ones who talk to me at least.'

'You're on.'

The meal's over. Bestégui gives a deep sigh.

'Fine, then I won't rush into it.'

Connivance, compromise, always treading a fine line.

♣

Katryn and Chardon part company in the street in front of the Brasserie des Sports. From a distance, Fernandez follows Katryn who walks very fast. She's wearing a long cream-coloured waterproof duster coat. She enters an upmarket apartment building on avenue Mathurin-Moreau. Fernandez draws nearer. She punches in the entry code for the front door. Her fingers leave grey smudges on four figures and a letter. He tries various random combinations; on the third, the door opens. He goes inside. Katryn is no longer in the lobby. The lift is on its way down. To the cellar, or the garage. It stops at the lower basement level. Instinctively, Fernandez follows. *I'll think of something.*

There's a dim light controlled by a timer switch and one of the lock-ups is open, two rows further back. Katryn drives out a red Mini, stops the car and gets out to close the door behind her. Fernandez moves closer. *She might recognise me.* He places his hand on her arm. Katryn over-reacts violently. She screams and punches him in the face with all her strength, hitting out wildly. Fernandez, caught unawares, protects himself as best he can.

'Stop ... I want to talk to you ...' Crushing her arm: 'Talk to you, do you hear, shit ...'

She's not listening, but carries on lashing out blindly, screaming. He pushes her into the lock-up, a hand over her mouth.

'Shut the fuck up.'

She bites him and draws blood. He releases her and she makes a dive for the open door of the car. *A whore ... That's why she's making trouble ...* He takes out his revolver with his right hand, to keep her quiet, grabs her again with his left hand and yanks her away from the car which she's clinging on to. She's hurt her hands. He pins her to the wall again, waves the revolver in front of her face, yelling:

'Calm down!'

Feeling the gun barrel at her throat, her whole body convulses, she shoots both her legs out at waist level, he doubles over and a shot is fired. Killed outright, Katryn slides along the wall.

The shot resonates for a long time. The sound mingles with the smell of gunpowder and burning petrol. Winded, Fernandez stares aghast, his heart thumping wildly.

The light timer cuts out and the only sound is the Mini's engine ticking over. He leans against the wall. *This killing means curtains for me. Unacceptable. A left-wing cop, the security branch, all the fun and games, my meeting with Bornand, the Élysée, a ten-year battle. He catches his breath. I'm not giving all that up. I need a few hours. Got to get going.*

He switches the light back on, gets behind the wheel of the car and drives it back into the lock-up. He closes the door. It's not the ideal shelter, there's another car, but even so it's better than leaving it wide open. The body lies crumpled on the ground right there in front of him. There's a streak of blood down the wall and a dark red pool is gradually spreading over the floor. *This is a total fuck-up. I can't leave her here, someone might find her any minute and identify her straight away, and I'm in the front line. I'll play for time and try and pin it on Chardon.*

He opens the car door and dumps the body on the passenger seat, turning it to one side as if the girl were asleep. He covers her with her long raincoat, rummages in her bag and finds the remote control for the garage. He takes a deep breath and drives the Mini out of the garage. Blood on his clothes and in the car. It's starting to snow. *That's probably good news, there'll be fewer nosey people about, but it's not possible to drive too far, too risky in this weather.*

Nearby in the 19th *arrondissement* there's a place that's deserted at this hour and in this weather – the La Villette automated parking lot. He heads in that direction, driving cautiously. He reaches the esplanade with its asphalt avenues divided by pavements fringed with bare trees. The street lamps are out. The snow's falling thick and fast and settling on the tarmac and on the branches of the trees. A glow comes from the ring road above the parking lot, and there are a few lights shining on the vast La Villette construction site a hundred metres away. Fernandez and his corpse are surrounded by a fuzzy black void. He pulls up alongside the row of shrubs and pines bordering the parking lot exit ramp, walks around the car, opens the passenger door, heaves the body onto the ground, nudges it under the bushes with his foot and covers it with the cream-coloured raincoat. Immediately the snow begins to obliterate the corpse. He glances around him, still nobody. In ten minutes, everything will be covered with snow. He gets back into the car, pays at the machine, and turns onto avenue Jean-Jaurès. He pauses to adjust the seat and the driving mirror, then stops by a telephone booth, rings directory inquiries for Chardon's number and calls him. *Oh God of all cops, please let him be home.* He's home.

'I'm a friend of Katryn's. She wants you to come and take some photos.'

'Don't say anything over the phone.'

'I'll come and pick you up outside your place in fifteen minutes. I've got Katryn's car.'

'OK.'

He buys a roll of kitchen paper, cleans up the most visible bloodstains in the car and puts Katryn's handbag in the boot. He places his revolver on the back seat concealed under his leather jacket and sets off.

Chardon lives in a house in a little dead-end street at the top of a hill. The snow makes driving really difficult. No cars, no pedestrians, everyone shut up indoors. Only some kids ducking behind parked cars are having a huge snowball fight, shrieking and yelling. Chardon is waiting for him by his front door, sheltering under the porch. He slithers his way over to the car and gets in beside Fernandez, more intrigued than suspicious.

'Katryn is in Aubervilliers where we'd planned to meet up. Completely by chance, she spotted the CEO of a major company with some young – very young – local kids, that's all she told me. She stayed there and sent me to fetch you.' A long silence.

'Have you got your camera?'

'Don't worry.'

Silence. Unease. Be quick.

'You'll see, we won't be long.'

The road surface is slippery. They weave acrobatically in and out of the cars moving at a crawl. *As long as Chardon keeps his eyes on the road, as long as he's afraid, he won't inspect either the car's interior or my trousers too closely.* The window's open, letting in icy draughts to dispel the smell of blood.

Porte d'Aubervilliers. Fernandez takes the road running alongside the Saint-Denis canal, pressing harder and harder on the accelerator. He crosses the canal via the Pont du Landy, then, without slowing down, turns sharply onto a barely tar-macked path. Chardon turns to him with a questioning look. Fernandez, driving in the ruts with his left hand on the wheel, grabs his revolver from under his jacket on the back seat with his right hand, raises the gun to Chardon's head and fires. The body slumps forward onto the dashboard and the passenger window shatters. Without stopping, still using his right hand, Fernandez thrusts the body down between the dashboard and the passenger seat then covers it with his jacket. *It's only a rough sort of camouflage, but we're not going far, and the people around here tend to keep themselves to themselves.* He drives over a muddy waste ground bordering the canal and lands back on tarmac, zigzags through some sordid side streets, drives under the motorway and the railway line and into a breaker's yard. He stops the Mini fifty metres from a Portakabin and honks the horn. A skinny young man in blue overalls stands in the doorway waiting for him. They shake hands.

'A car for the crusher. And no looking inside.'

'Have you informed the boss?'

'Didn't have time. It's an emergency.'

The young man points to the telephone, inside the cabin.

'You have to. I don't take the decisions here.'

Fernandez calls. The boss is there. The young man turns on the loudspeaker.

'I need to dispose of a car, and it's urgent.'

'Full?'

'Partly, yes.'

'You know it'll cost you?'

'I've always paid, and always returned the favour.'

'OK.'

The young man heads over to the crusher, at the far end of the yard. Fernandez goes back to the Mini, removes Chardon's keys from his pockets and Katryn's key and diary from her handbag. Reluctantly he leaves his own soft leather jacket lined with sealskin on the front seat, but he can't afford to make any mistakes, then drives the car over to the crusher. He gets out and watches it being crunched. When a small car is flattened, it becomes like a pancake, a giant pancake, dripping with petrol, oil and blood, thrown into a tipper truck with other crushed vehicles. Fernandez feels relieved of a burden. *I've never heard of any corpse coming back from here.*

Time: five thirty. It's pitch dark. The yard's about to close. *And my day's not over. Metro, rush hour, keep a low profile.* Back home, he removes his clothes and stuffs them into a plastic bag. *Throw everything away.* He has a quick shower and dresses in similar style clothes – jeans and a leather jacket. Then he jumps into his car and races over to Chardon's place.

He parks at the bottom of the hill and walks up. It's still snowing but the kids have all gone home. He walks slowly, carrying out a recce. Railings and a half-open iron gate. He enters a small garden overgrown with ivy and shrubs covered with a blanket of snow which shield him from prying eyes. A two-storey brick house. The curtains haven't been drawn and no lights are on: the place looks empty. The key turns easily in the lock. But what if there's an alarm … the door opens, not a sound. He slips inside, closes the door behind him and begins to explore. The rooms are bathed in a faint orange glow from the street lights, striped by the curtain of steadily falling snow. *Take care to stay away from the windows.*

On the ground floor there's a junk room, a garage with a freezer, washing machine and workbench, and a locked door. It takes him a few moments to find the right key. He switches on the light to discover a windowless room that turns out to be a well-equipped photographer's darkroom. Everything is neat and tidy. Two photos are hanging from a line, drying, presumably taken by Chardon just before he went off for a drive. Two porn scenes, with people Fernandez recognises. He pockets them. They'll enjoy these at the Élysée. He switches off the light and goes upstairs.

The entire floor is taken up by one big, sparsely decorated room with windows on two sides, a Moroccan wool rug on the floor, and designer furniture: sofas, armchairs, a solid wood table – opulent comfort. Against one of the walls is a half-empty wall unit with a television, video recorder, hi-fi, records and cassettes. There's a state-of-the-art open-plan kitchen. A coffee pot on the hob, a dirty cup in the sink. Otherwise, the place is immaculately tidy. *Nothing for me here, don't waste time.*

On the second floor is a bedroom, office and bathroom. *Try the office first, makes sense.* An antique writing desk standing against one wall has been left open. Two piles of coloured folders. Fernandez flicks through the files quickly. The left-hand pile is all income tax, payslips, social security. Move on. The right-hand pile contains a few handwritten sheets, names, addresses, dates, memos probably, hardly of any interest. Chardon's archives must be stored somewhere else, at his bank perhaps, which would explain why there's so little protection. In the middle of the pile, there's a thicker folder. The first sheet of paper is a photocopy of the flight plan for a Boeing 747, Brussels-Zavantem-Valetta-Tehran, Thursday, 28 November 1985. Bingo. Easy. For a blackmailer, this guy's got no sense of security. Fernandez grabs the whole thing, fast. He places Katryn's diary and keys in one of the desk drawers, having wiped them carefully, aware that it's not very convincing. But he's improvising as he goes along, and he can't hang around for ever. Back in the hall, he waits a few moments, still not a sound in the street – the compelling silence of a snow-covered city. He leaves the house, slamming the door behind him, and walks off, turning up his jacket collar.

♣

Bornand's afternoon continues to be busy. At some point, Customs may decide to poke their noses into the business about the plane. So it's vital to talk to the Finance Minister.

But relations between the two men are complicated, fraught with stumbling blocks. He must prepare the ground. Timsit is the man of the moment. A graduate from the elite École Nationale d'Administration from which civil servants are drawn, his culture is very different from Bornand's and he has a great deal of influence on the government. They'd met several times on hunts organised by the Parillaud bank and talked at length about collectors' guns, and Bornand had offered him some magnificent specimens from Lebanon.

'I wanted to make a point of informing you before talking to the Minister about it. An arms deal with Iran. Nothing to do with big bucks, it's to do with secret negotiations over the release of the hostages. I've just come out of the President's office. He wants this business to be hushed up at all costs.'

Message received.

So at last to Flandin, the boss of the SEA, the applied electronics company that covered the deal. The tone is not the same as it was last night. Bornand finds him jittery, anxious to protect his company at all costs. There's the rub, most likely.

'I warn you, no way will I carry the can. Do what you need to do to stifle this thing, otherwise I'll spill the beans on all the lousy payoffs from the Iran deals, yours for starters. And I'm not picking up the tab on my own.'

Bornand reclines in his armchair and stretches out his legs. If things get more complicated, this guy will soon become a problem. *The minute I chose to work with a novice on this type of deal, I was taking a risk and I knew it. I'll give Beauchamp a call and tell him it's time to shut him up. After all, that's what I brought him into the SEA security service for.* A half smile. To win you have to be one step ahead of the game.

Fernandez is back. Bornand pours two whiskies and leafs through the dossier he's given him. The entire operation is set out. Well, not quite. The particulars of last February's decision by the armaments division of the Defence Ministry: the air force's Matra Magic 550 missiles are to be replaced by a more efficient model. In May, there's the contract between the armaments division and a company specialising in electronic equipment, the SEA, which purchases the missiles for the sum of five million francs and pledges to disable them and recycle the onboard equipment in the civil aviation sector. The missiles are delivered to the SEA's hangars in September. In October, the SEA sells electronic equipment to SAPA, a financial company registered in the Bahamas, for the sum of 30 million francs. The same day, SAPA sells the same equipment on to SICI, a Malta-based company, for the sum of 40 million francs. The equipment is loaded at Brussels International (Zavantem) Airport, destined for SICI, in Malta. The flight plan of the Boeing 747 carrying the equipment clearly shows that the plane never landed in Malta but diverted to Tehran. A separate sheet also shows that two weeks ago, Camoc, a Lebanese company specialising in recycling and adapting French, American and Israeli weapons, opened a branch in Tehran. In short, the entire chain is there, all ready to be spoon-fed to the press, it'll be all too easy for them to check it out.

Bornand looks up at Fernandez:

'Terrific work, young man. I daren't ask you how you got hold of this ...'

He smiles.

'Chardon and Katryn left the restaurant together, quite late, around three, after a game of snooker, and from what I was able to overhear, they were off to a meeting together with someone in Paris. It's perfectly simple, I took advantage to go and check out Chardon's place. I took the dossier, because I thought it might make him stop and think twice.'

Bornand raises his glass to him and nods. Fernandez continues:

'Among Chardon's files, I also found some photos. Jean-Pierre Tardivel, an influential journalist at *Combat Présent*, the far-right weekly, having a bit of fun with two exceedingly young boys ...'

He nudges the photo towards Bornand who leans forward attentively:

'That's extremely interesting. I'll keep it. I'm sure it'll come in useful.'

'... and the fabulous Delia Paxton being fucked by two drag queens, in a setting that looks like a porn shoot.'

Bornand takes the photo and slides it into an envelope.

'For the President. He's a fan of Delia Paxton, he goes to see all her films incognito, on the biggest screens possible. At least now he'll know what to talk about when he meets her at a dinner party. Or in his speech when he awards her the Legion of Honour.'

After Fernandez has left, Bornand pours himself another whisky. Silence in the night. Just a disk of coloured light on the desktop. He needs time to mull things over.

Whoever built up this dossier has sources at every level of the operation, within the ministerial department, at the SEA, but also inside Camoc in Beirut, whose involvement is largely unknown back here. The only two people in Paris who are aware of its involvement are the boss of the SEA and myself. It would probably be easier to track them in Beirut than here. Beirut ... Moricet.

Flashback: Moricet tall, built like a fighter, a seducer's smile on the face of a pirate, and a quirky taste in clothes with a penchant for elegant linen suits. Both high on cocaine in a hazily remembered Beirut brothel with fluid outlines, a luxury apartment gutted by the war, and a stupid competition: which of them could fuck the most girls in two hours? And Moricet had won with nine to his six. Age had certainly been against Bornand, but in any case, he put up a respectable performance.

Another flashback: Moricet and himself, totally hammered, in Beirut, in an unknown car, hemmed in by two groups of armed men. Sobering up in a flash, Moricet had pushed him to the floor of the car, then speeding forward, shooting with a gun that had appeared from nowhere, bullets ricocheting off the bodywork, had got them out of there. Then Moricet drove him back to the Christian quarter. The memory of being scared shitless, the kind of fear that makes you feel you're really living, and a friend he knew he could rely on.

'Attempted kidnapping plus a demand for ransom,' Moricet had commented dryly. 'The most profitable industry in this country since the war started.'

'More profitable than the bank, I fear.'

And he had confided some of his concerns over the International Bank of Lebanon, the IBL, which was well established in the Christian community but since the start of the war had been losing its customers among the other Lebanese religious communities, the Syrians, and the rest of the Middle East.

'Negotiate with the Syrians.'

'We'd like to, but it's not easy. They're more than a little wary of us.'

'I know the head of the Syrian secret services. Do you want to meet him?'

Two days later, he was as good as his word. A long conversation about the latest archaeological research in Syria (my passion, the secret service man had told them), which Bornand had contributed to as best he could. Honourably, it would appear, since the Syrian came to visit him in Paris each time he was in France on unofficial business, and some of his friends had been appointed to the board of the IBL, which had picked up again. As a matter of fact, that had been a major turning point in the bank's fortunes. Moricet, a man of action.

In 1982, Bornand had invited him to join the Élysée unit. Which he had done, but not for long: 'Too many nutters,' he said, 'too many bureaucrats, too many bosses, not enough action or sun.' And he'd set up his own private security firm, ISIS, based in Beirut and which operated throughout the Middle East. If you want to find out something about Camoc, Moricet is definitely your man.

Telephone. He'll be there tomorrow.

Bornand carefully puts away his notes in one of the two cupboards. Amid the ornate arabesques and carved acanthus leaves are records of everything that has been said in this office, accumulated over four years, a real treasure trove. He locks the cupboard then pours himself one last whisky, which he knocks back standing by the window gazing out over the rooftops.

♣

Fernandez finds himself back in the street. It's still snowing. Gone, the warmth of the office, the whisky and Bornand. He's exhausted. He has no desire to go back home and be alone with his dead. He enters the nearest café, orders a Calvados, goes into the toilet and does a line of coke. Good feeling. To be honest, if you think about it, the situation is rather funny. Finish the night off at Mado's, Katryn's boss. Brilliant idea. What class.

On the ground floor of Mado's building is a vast bar with English-style decor and a hushed, sophisticated atmosphere. Fernandez, Bornand's right-hand man, has free access to the whole place. The barman greets him and pours him a brandy, which he downs in one, then he goes downstairs to the basement. Swingers' club. Among a certain bourgeois clientele it's the new fad; sounds better than going to a prostitute, but it's no different, except there are a few non-professionals. Mado's real clientele to whom she owes her fame and fortune, the ones who have a great deal of money and a great deal of power, prefer the call girl network and orgies in the first-floor lounges.

In the half-dark, there's a musty smell of sweat and sex, claustrophobia and dust, and the music has an insistent, deafening beat. Fernandez relaxes. Two women rigged out in various items of spiky armour are dancing in a corner. Elsewhere, scantily clad men and women grind rhythmically against each other. On the fringes, couples are entangled on sofas in the alcoves. Girls everywhere, within arm's reach, available, accessible. Fernandez is suddenly fascinated by a girl who's dancing naked in the spotlight, with exaggerated movements. A smooth, round arse, engaging but not aggressive, two huge white breasts jiggling and, above them, her head covered with a helmet of black hair, cut over the ears. She has no face. No face. It touches a raw nerve. Flashback: Katryn's head in the darkness of the garage, thrust against the wall, screaming, the back of her neck exploding. Against a background of hypnotic music.

He walks over to the girl and grabs her arm, drags her to

an alcove and tries to part her hair. No face, just a mouth that opens, a silent chasm. A punch to shut that mouth, two, three, a scuffle, Fernandez crumples, stunned by two beefy bouncers amid the general confusion.

Mado, summoned urgently, has him taken to one of the first-floor bedrooms. The victim has a split lip and a nasty cut over her eye. A doctor is called to tend to her immediately. Really bad luck, the girl was one of the few non-professionals there that night. She groans, threatening to report Fernandez.

'This guy's a nutter,' says Mado, very motherly, and surreptitiously mentions damages.

'A nutter for sure. He was screaming "Catherine, Catherine". My name's not Catherine, he couldn't hear a thing. He started hitting me.' Her body quivers with sobs. 'Scared the life out of me.'

'Katryn,' says Mado, suddenly pensive, tidying the young woman's black hair matted with blood and sweat with her fingertips.

Katryn, a model of professionalism, who'd let her down this evening, for the first time since she'd been working for her.

♣

Bornand, in a black dinner jacket, is reclining on a chaise longue in his mistress's bedroom, which is done out in green and white with blonde wood Louis-Philippe-style furniture. On his left are two high windows with the curtains open, overlooking the Champ-de-Mars. Through the lattice of snow-covered trees, he can see the Eiffel Tower illuminated, a tangle of girders glinting copper in the light, emphasised by the white snow, the familiar presence of the technological dream shrouded in nostalgia. A wave of tiredness. Shooting pains in the palm of his right hand, and each time the fleeting image of a pool of blood spreading uncontrollably. A tough day. The President dreaming of the Académie Française, Bestégui stuffing himself, Fernandez a petty housebreaker. And earlier, the reception at the Embassy. He feels ground down. He's come here to recover, in the calm surroundings of her boudoir. Put a greater distance between himself and all the stress. From his pocket he takes out a gold and black lacquered case, carefully selects a cigarette, a mix of angel dust and marijuana, lights it and takes a long drag. An almost instant sense of well-being. He contemplates his mistress, sitting naked on a low stool at the dressing table, carrying out the ritual she performs for him. He can see three-quarters of her back and her full frontal reflection in the big mirror. A Degas painting. He takes a second drag, holds the smoke in for a long time, and slowly exhales. The image of the young woman shimmers and dissolves. Another face fleetingly appears, that of a very young girl. He creases his eyes to capture it. Too late, it disperses with a metallic sound. He stubs out his cigarette.

Her blonde hair is piled up in a sophisticated chignon, showing off the nape of her neck and the outline of her shoulders. He is utterly absorbed in watching each of her slow, accomplished movements. First of all, she applies foundation, almost lazily, like a sort of slow preliminary, then the tension increases, a few dabs to touch up under the eyes, around the cheekbones. She surveys the overall effect, and her gaze is drawn towards the mirror, intense, her torso slightly inclined, her arms raised, her breasts swell, lolling forward too, her back elongates, her hips spread. She outlines her eyes with precise strokes, paints her mouth (he loves the way she pinches her lips together), highlights her cheekbones, hollows out her cheeks, makes a correction here and there. A refined, artificial world that exists only for him. He gently caresses his half-erection.

The application of the mask is complete.

'We're going to be late,' she says without turning round, glancing at the reflection of the man in black in the corner of the mirror.

'It doesn't matter. Take your time.'

'I don't feel like going out this evening.'

He looks away. She sighs, rises, slips on ivory silk stockings, a magic moment when her living flesh is transformed into a smooth, perfect shimmering shape. He closes his eyes. Good, very good. Then the long dress, crimson like her lips, fluid over her body, flared at the hem, long sleeves covering her shoulders and a V-neck that plunges to her waist, her breasts unfettered beneath the fabric. Matching high-heeled shoes, the superb arch of her feet, sophisticated balance. She leans over her dressing table, takes a pair of gold earrings from the drawer and puts them on, then a necklace. 'No need,' he says and she turns around. He gets up and from his pocket produces a velvet box. He opens it and takes out a round object made of gold. Françoise accepts it, running her finger over the chasing: a geometric design depicting a curled-up panther in unpolished beaten gold. There's something strange and savage about it.

'Exquisite. Where does it come from?'

'From the wilds of the steppes, from the depths of time. The minute I saw it, I wanted it for you. I had it mounted.' He goes over to her and fastens the necklace around her neck. 'I could picture you wearing it just like this, with this dress.'

He kisses her hair, moves his lips down to her ear which

he brushes with his moustache, takes the earring between his teeth, tastes the coolness of the metal, and pulls gently. She moves away, smiles at him and winks: 'Very fragile, this work of art, don't touch,' then urges:

'Let's stay here this evening, I don't feel like going out.'

He holds out her coat, envelops her in it, keeps his arms around her and caresses her face with the fur collar.

'What you feel like is of little importance, my beauty.'

Saturday 30 November

There is something sinister about the parking lot at La Villette at eight o'clock in the morning, in the middle of winter, bathed in the orange glow of the big city. The gleaming wet black tarmac, divided into long strips by granite pavements and marked off with white lines and puny saplings forms a desolate geometric universe a stone's throw from the construction sites of La Villette. Two cop cars are parked in a corner, blue lights flashing and headlights glaring. The cops, four in uniform, two in plain clothes, are huddled by a row of shrubs. A Caribbean-looking man wearing a woollen hat and scarf and a leather bomber jacket is holding his wolfhound on a leash and pointing to a human form lying under the scrawny bushes.

The two plainclothes cops approach. Noria Ghozali, small and muffled inside a cheap black anorak, stands slightly back, behind Inspector Bonfils, a young trainee she's working with for the first time. Instinctively, she's on her guard: a man, her superior, she's wary.

Bonfils leans over. The body is almost entirely covered by a cream-coloured raincoat. He touches the protruding wrist and hand. Cold, very cold. Gingerly he lifts the raincoat. A woman's body lying on her stomach, black trousers and sweater, her face turned to one side, almost intact, her eyes closed, the back of her neck split open. All that's left is a dark brown depression of soft matter, with splinters of greyish bone and matted hair. And under her chin, in her throat, the clean, clear impact of a bullet. Nothing spectacular, thinks Bonfils, surprisingly unaffected. A used thing lying there as if it had been thrown out a long time ago. He straightens up and turns to the uniformed cops:

'Death from a gunshot wound. Call the station and the prosecutor.'

Then he takes out his notebook and continues:

'Now, Mr Saint-André, tell me how you came across the body?'

'I live on the other side of the ring road.'

'Where, to be precise?'

'36 rue Hoche, in Pantin.'

'Go on.'

'Every morning, I take my dog for a walk around the parking lot, or along the canal, before leaving for work. I also work on Saturdays, you know.'

'Where do you work?'

'Maintenance, at the Galeries Lafayette.' A pause. 'Anyway, this morning, it was the parking lot. My dog found the body at around a quarter to eight, or thereabouts.'

'What happened?'

'He was running ahead of me and he stopped by the bushes and started growling and tugging at something, the shoe, I think. I thought he'd found a dead animal and went over to fetch him back, and that was it. Then I ran to avenue Jean-Jaurès, called the police from a phone box, and I waited for you at the parking lot entrance.'

'Did your dog move the body?'

'No, he didn't have time. I'm very fond of my dog, so I'm careful about what he eats. No rotting carcases.'

'Do you only come here in the morning?'

'Yes. At night, I just take him round the block, I'm tired, you understand …'

'Did you meet anyone when you were out walking this morning?'

'No, not today or any other morning. That's why I come here, because I can let my dog off the lead without bothering anyone. Anywhere else and people always yell at you.'

'What about yesterday morning?'

'I went along the canal. Every other day, for a bit of variety.'

After repeating his contact details, Saint-André leaves with his dog.

Ghozali and Bonfils pace up and down side by side to keep warm. He's broad-shouldered and much taller than her. Wearing a flying jacket that fits snugly over the hips, he looks elegant, laid-back. He takes out a pack of filter-tipped Gauloises from his pocket and offers her a cigarette.

'No thanks, I don't smoke.'

'You're very quiet.'

'I'm watching you work.'

He exhales the smoke, savouring the first puff. The note of aggression in her voice doesn't escape him. He shoots her a sidelong glance. Strange little woman, hair drawn back into a severe bun, a round, slightly flat face, not exactly attractive. But there's a sort of fierceness locked in behind that concrete wall. He continues:

'You know, this is my first posting, my first day on duty, and my first corpse. You won't learn much from watching me.' He pauses for thought. 'I think I was expecting something more shocking.'

'Are you disappointed?'

He smiles.

'That's one way of putting it.'

The Crime Squad arrives. Suits and ties, overcoats, elegant leather shoes. Polite, distant, busy and competent. At once the machine goes into motion. Bonfils makes his report, Ghozali, standing back slightly, listens. The parking lot is surrounded, cordoned off, the area around explored. The forensic team arrives, dressed in white overalls, and sets to work. Noria watches them, fascinated. Bonfils turns to her:

'Are you coming? We're going back to the station.'

She blurts out angrily, her face inscrutable:

'You go back, I'm staying. To watch the real professionals at work.'

Her words hang in the air. A silence.

'Right. I'll tell the superintendent that you were needed here.'

Noria watches him walk off, puzzled. Could this man be different from the others?

Photos. Noria picks up a Polaroid of the dead woman's face. Pathologist. A few simple movements of the body. Initial conclusions. Killed by a bullet through the neck, shot at close range, but not here. The body was dumped here very shortly after the murder, which took place about fifteen hours ago or a little more, hard to say at first glance, given the snow and the drop in temperature. Probably driven here. The lab tests will yield more precise information. No ID on the body. A very big pearl pendant, that might be useful later. No marks, no footprints on the tarmac or in the flower bed, seemingly no witnesses, until the building workers have been questioned. If she's not reported missing, identification won't be easy. Noria takes note. An ambulance takes the body away, and the parking lot gradually empties.

At nine a.m., Nicolas Martenot rings the bell of Bornand's apartment. The door is opened by a manservant wearing a black open-necked shirt, sleeves rolled up, black trousers (*I've always wondered what Bornand gets up to with a good-looking guy like that*), who shows him into the drawing room and takes his coat:

'Monsieur Bornand will be down shortly.'

Martenot goes over to the French window that opens onto a lawn enclosed by ivy-covered railings. On the other side is the Champ-de-Mars, all very peaceful. A glance at the Eiffel Tower, with its dark tangle of girders. He returns to the drawing room. Eighteenth-century blonde wood panelling, Versailles oak parquet floor. On the wall facing the French windows is a magnificent Canaletto, the *Grand Canal in front of the Doge's Palace*. The painting has great elegance, the gondoliers' silhouettes leaning over their oars and the froth on the surface of the green lagoon captured in a few brushstrokes. Beside it, three small scenes of Venetian life by Pietro Longhi, hung asymmetrically, look very flat. And, against the wall, a rare piece of furniture, a seat designed by Gaudí, in carved wood, extremely light and elaborate. Martenot gazes at it with a twinge of envy. On the right, a Louis XV marble fireplace. He goes over to the log fire, which is very pleasant in this damp weather. On the mantelpiece is the marble head of a Greek ephebe. He caresses its cheek with the back of his hand, relishing the smooth, cold feel. Opposite it, a terracotta statuette of a Cretan goddess with bulging eyes and a heavy, ankle-length robe, her arms outstretched and her hands clutching bundles of snakes. Above the fireplace hangs a portrait of Dora Maar by Picasso. In front of it is a vast sofa, two massive square armchairs upholstered in white and an ornate, inlaid low Chinese table standing on a Persian rug in varying hues of red.

He feels as if he has always known this impeccably furnished, unchanging, almost lifeless room. A decor designed as a showcase for Bornand's wealth and culture. Only the snake goddess lent a rare note of incongruity.

He'd come here for the first time more than twenty years ago with his father, a brilliant defence lawyer who'd made a name for himself after the war defending collaborators. This stocky man with crew-cut hair and a grating voice who resembled a wild boar was Bornand's close friend. And for Bornand, friendship was sacred. A friend is for life, whatever he does. And Nicolas Martenot inherited this friendship, along with the rest of his legacy. He has attended dozens of gatherings in this drawing room, no grand receptions, but meetings with handpicked associates, personal bonds forming, networks being reinforced, with Bornand at the centre, at the hub of the power machine, elegant and controlling. An instrument of power, and the thrill that goes with it.

Five or six years back, not that long ago and right here in this very room, Bornand had introduced him to his Iranian friends, a few months after the overthrow of the Shah, in the middle of the US Embassy hostage crisis. Two men in their forties, Harvard graduates, in dark suits, equally at ease with the Canaletto and the Picasso. They headed up the international pool of lawyers brought in to support the Iranian government in the countless international disputes resulting from the Islamic revolution. Being part of this pool changed his life, introducing him into the business world operating at planetary level, and making his law firm one of the most prominent in

Paris, with branches in ten countries. It also made him a fully-fledged member of Bornand's 'family', and it was to Bornand he partly owed his wealth.

Martenot turns around, Bornand's slim figure has just entered the room. He's sporting a beige polo-neck sweater with leather elbow patches, brown velvet trousers and worn tawny leather moccasins. He walks over to Nicolas, puts his arm around his shoulders and hugs him briefly. There's a great deal of affection in his gesture. Then he turns to the manservant:

'Bring us some coffee, Antoine, and then you may leave.'

A fine porcelain tray bearing pastries and chocolates. Relaxed, Bornand pours the coffee then sinks into an armchair.

'When did you get back from Tehran?'

'Last night, at around ten.'

'Well?'

'It's not good news.'

'As I feared.'

'My trip was timed to coincide with the first missile deliveries. The disappearance of the plane caused mayhem.' Bornand listens closely but says nothing. 'I met our friends, separately, then all together. They're unanimous: there's nothing left to negotiate. You've been aware of their demands in return for freeing the hostages for nearly a year, and still nothing. They're beginning to doubt that you're in a position to break the deadlock in Paris. Especially as the RPR right-wing opposition party sent an envoy to Tehran, a certain Antonelli, do you know him?' Bornand nods. 'I haven't met him, obviously, but I've kept a close eye on him. He's offering the Iranians better loan repayment conditions and arms deals after the RPR wins the March election, providing they refuse to negotiate with us now.'

'The Iranians aren't stupid. They're only too aware that the Gaullists have always had a special relationship with Iraq, that they negotiated major arms deals and the contract to build Iraq's nuclear power station. They can't rely on pre-election promises.'

'They see the sabotage of the plane as the result of French political infighting ...'

'They're not wrong.'

'... and to be honest, they've had enough. In a nutshell, they're giving you two weeks to progress their demands in a visible and public way, otherwise, they'll break off all contact until the much heralded election of March '86. And bye-bye hostages.'

'An ultimatum?'

'Exactly. Can you meet it?'

Bornand thinks long and hard, his eyes half closed, rubbing the palm of his left hand. A sharp, stimulating pain. Nicolas watches him carefully.

'Well, François?'

Bornand sits up.

'Two weeks isn't long.'

'But why, why? You know as well as I do that Iraq is on its last legs and will never pay for the arms we supply. Iran is winning the war financially. There's a rapprochement between Saudi Arabia and Tehran, and the Saudis want a war with no winner and no loser. Why the delay? Not to mention the Americans. Or rather yes, let's mention them. In Tehran, I met Green. His room was next to mine ...'

'That can't be a coincidence ...'

'We played poker all night, and he won.'

'A bad sign.'

'They're going to be stepping up their deliveries of arms to Iran, with the blessing of Saudi Arabia and Israel.'

'But not of the American Congress.'

Martenot smiles.

'As you can imagine, it didn't seem to worry Green. And what about us? Why can't we simply review our policy on Iran? That's the President's intention.'

'I know, I know. But political life is becoming paralysed in the run-up to the election.'

'A rather feeble explanation, and you know it.'

'True ... Well let's say there's a clan-based power system here in France, and a President who is no longer able to arbitrate, to decide, when issues are as complicated as they are in the Middle East ...'

'And when there are such huge financial interests at stake. The French arms dealers who've invested billions in Iraq know full well that they'll never be paid if Baghdad loses the war.'

'Naturally, that's another factor. In other words, it's hard to get things moving, but I'll manage it, and that's a promise. I'm simply saying that two weeks isn't long enough.'

Martenot rises.

'It feels like the writing's on the wall for this government.'

Bornand smiles.

'There's an element of that. Trust me.' He sees Martenot to the door. 'I'll keep you posted.'

On the first floor, in the green and white bedroom of Bornand's mistress, Françoise Michel, Nicolas is reclining naked on the vast white duvet covering the bed. In the centre of the room is the chaise longue, and to the right, the dressing table beneath a giant mirror. Françoise comes in, wearing a green silk tea-gown, tied at the waist, her long, almost straight blonde hair cascading down to her hips. She sashays over to the chaise longue, stops, unties her dress and, turning slowly around, with a languid, deliberate gesture, lets it slide to the floor in a pool of colour and gathers up her hair and twists it into a knot at the base of her neck. She's the focus of every pair of eyes, in charge, sovereign. The curtains have been drawn across the windows, two uplighters illuminate the ceiling. Nicolas gazes at her sinuous white body in this shadowless light, he loves this exaggerated *mise en scène*. Bornand's mistress, stolen, shared. He has a hard-on. She turns to him and stretches out her leg. He kneels before her, removes one white mule and then the other, traces the shape of her foot with his hand, and then her leg, with a precise movement, up to her knee where he places his lips. Her skin is cool and gives off a fragrance of sweet almond. *I'm hunting on his ground.* His hand moves up to her thigh and he buries his face in her blonde pubic hair, seeks her crotch, finds it soft, alive, a powerful, intense taste. His preserve. He's gripped by a violent desire. Françoise, present and remote, opens her thighs or pushes him away, grips him, eludes him, derives pleasure from toying with his feelings, she who prides herself in having none, and letting him know it. Only the almost abstract thrill at the spectacle she's putting on for Bornand, standing behind the two-way mirror. Perhaps.

And suddenly desire wells up in her belly, completely overwhelms her, submerges her, taking her right out of herself. She wants to scream, bites her lip and draws blood. She grabs Nicolas's head, jerks him out of her cunt, thrusts his shoulders back, pinning him to the ground, and beats her fists against him, her face masked by her hair that has come loose. She crushes him under her weight, straddles him, moves up and down with fury and hatred, until he comes, trembling and groaning. Then she spits in his face, steps over him, gathers up her green gown and leaves him alone, lying on the floor, breathless, adrift, under the gaze of Bornand, helpless. Nicolas gives a seismic shudder.

Françoise locks herself in her bathroom. A chill in her bones, her lip swollen, her cunt, her belly painful and throbbing, her heart racing. Was Bornand there, behind the mirror? A growing doubt which spreads outward through sharp stabbing pains in her belly. Guilty. Her heart thumps, blood rushes to her temples. Go back, submit to his dry, authoritarian hand. Her head's swimming. She runs a hot bath, with lots of foam, slides into it, lights a joint, inhales deeply, her eyes closed, and slowly regains her equilibrium. *Above all, don't try to understand. Forget. Shut out Bornand. At least for the time being. Let your mind go blank. Look forward to a long weekend with the family.*
   Wait until tomorrow.

♣

Noria turns into avenue Jean-Jaurès and heads for the police station, walking very slowly. An unknown woman, not easy to identify. If she's not identified, it won't be possible to carry out an inquest. She wasn't killed on the spot. It's one hell of a gamble, dumping a body in an open-air public parking lot with a building site nearby. Even after dark, there might be people around. Premise: the murderer acted in a hurry. A body on his hands, nothing planned, got to get rid of it. Premise: in that case, you don't drive all the way across Paris to throw a body onto the La Villette parking lot. You dump it as nearby as possible. So, it's [highly?] likely that the woman was killed locally. If she was killed locally, it's [fairly?] likely that she lives or works in the neighbourhood. And in that case, it's [just?] likely that someone local knows her and might recognise her. She fingers the leather card wallet in her pocket in which she'd tucked the photo of the dead woman next to her cop ID. *This is my patch. If that person's out there, I can find them.*

The 19th *arrondissement* police headquarters is almost deserted at this hour. No one says a word to her and that suits her fine. Bonfils has already gone home, leaving her a copy of his report. She adds a few lines, looks out a large-scale map of the area, folds it, puts it in her pocket and walks home.

Rue Piat, halfway down rue de Belleville, is deserted in this freezing weather. The narrow street, its pavements spattered with dirty slush from the melting snow, glistens with a dampness that permeates your lungs. Set back on the left, is a huge social housing block, at least ten storeys high, with a flat, uniform façade, the very worst of urban architecture, typical of the unbridled renovation of the Belleville district begun back in the 1970s. Noria enters the staircase C lobby with its chipped concrete, graffiti and pungent smells. She's perfectly at home, this is the backdrop to her childhood. She closes her eyes and lets her mind go blank as she crosses the lobby.

She takes the lift to the eighth floor and opens the door to her studio flat with a sigh of contentment, removes her anorak and boots and walks barefoot over the floorboards to the window. A stunning view over the city spread out below and changing like the sea. Today it is a dull, monotonous grey, bounded to the west by the dark outline of the Meudon forest and Mont Valérien, with Montmartre rising up on the right, directly facing the geometric concrete mass of La Défense. The sky is still light, night slowly envelops the streets and buildings, all's well with the world.

She unpins her chignon with a swift movement, letting her glossy black hair tumble over her shoulders. She shakes her head and relishes a wonderful relaxing sensation. She feels almost rested already. Her place, with a mattress on the floor for a bed, covered by heavy burgundy-coloured blanket, a few paperbacks on a metal shelf, her bathtub, a real one, a luxury, and her tiny kitchen. Nobody to monopolise the bathroom, block up the toilet or stop her from reading or lazing around. Or even breathing.

She removes her clothes, dropping them haphazardly onto the floor, pulls on a shapeless knee-length T-shirt, grabs a packet of biscuits and lies on her stomach on her mattress, pencil in hand with the map of the area spread out on the floor in front of her. This map is alive, Noria has roamed every one of its streets, watching people passing by, keen to catch a look, an expression, a movement, inventing amazing stories for each of them, conducting imaginary conversations, sometimes following them, sometimes recognising them, taming this piece of the city where she works, no longer the solitary outsider. She locates the nerve centres, those intersections where shops, cafés, tobacconists, newspaper kiosks and metro entrances are concentrated, on which the inhabitants of the surrounding streets converge daily along set routes. She traces the catchment area around each of them, the dividing lines whose boundaries are hazy. Rue de Belleville, near where she lives, divided between place des Fêtes, Jourdain and lower Belleville … Barely an hour's work, recalling her endless walks almost step by step. And now, this is her opportunity. She mustn't let it slip.

She stares at her map, daydreams a little. Where to begin? Tomorrow's Sunday, there'll be crowds of people at the markets and in the streets where the food shops are concentrated. She pictures the body again. A slim woman, with elaborately manicured hands, despite her grazes, very simple but classy clothes, especially the long, well-cut, cream-coloured raincoat of expensive fabric, and the large pearl, an unusual piece of jewellery. Don't look in the more working-class parts of the neighbourhood, rather in the upmarket area, around the Buttes Chaumont park. *I'll start in the market on rue de Meaux, and I'll come back up to the Buttes via Laumière.* She feels a sort of elation.

❦

Françoise has locked herself in upstairs, incommunicado. Bornand, in his drawing room on the ground floor, pours himself a whisky, selects a hash cigarette with a few pinches of angel dust and ensconces himself in his armchair by the log fire. Dreamily he contemplates the statuette of the serpent goddess on the mantelpiece, as her contours become blurred. All he's aware of are her inlaid eyes and her menacing energy.

The doorbell clangs and Bornand jumps. He must have dozed off. Antoine has left. He rises and opens the door to Moricet and shows him into the lounge. The same as ever, tall, square, his hair very short, jutting jaw and thin lips, a laid-back street-fighter. He walks over to one of the French windows and glances out at the Eiffel Tower, then warms himself at the fire.

'How was Beirut this morning?'

'Beautiful weather, not as wet as here, and quiet, incredibly quiet since yesterday. Not a shot. It's surprising.'

'Would you like something to eat or drink?'

'I'd love something, whatever you've got to hand. Airline food's not exactly …'

Bornand wanders into the kitchen and comes back with smoked salmon sandwiches and vodka, which he sets down on the low table.

'I need you, Jean-Pierre.'

'That's why I'm here.'

Bornand reflects for a moment, kneading the palm of his left hand which twinges, as if to keep himself awake. Moricet sits on the sofa and bites into a sandwich.

'A plane vanished yesterday in mid-flight over Turkey. It was carrying arms to Iran. A delivery in which I'm implicated and which was financed by the IBL.' Moricet patiently waits for the rest to follow. 'I want to know who was behind it.'

'Can't you guess? Off the top of my head I'd say – and I'm pretty sure I'm right – the Iraqis and their supplier friends in France. Unless I'm mistaken, Thomson, Dassault, Matra, the Société Nationale Industrielle Aérospatiale, practically the entire French arms industry. What do you expect, it's war. Write it off as a loss.'

'It's not just a matter of competition between arms dealers. There's political capital to be made out of this affair here in France. There's a dossier circulating among the Parisian news-paper editors with evidence of clandestine arms deals with Iran, and I believe that the aim is to destabilise the Socialists before the March election.'

Moricet gazes at him over his sandwich.

'And you're likely to lose face as well as money.'

'And I'm going to lose face.'

'What do you intend to do?'

'If I find out exactly who's behind this campaign, and pin down names, facts, I can try and stop it, or at least negotiate as far as possible, conduct a damage limitation exercise.'

'And what do you want from me?'

'I need to check the reliability of a company in Beirut.'

'Shoot.'

'Camoc is based in the Halat airfield district. They carry out repairs and maintenance on all sorts of weapons.'

'I know them.'

'We commissioned them to adapt the American aircraft equipment the Iranians bought from us.'

'When?'

'Initial contact in April, implementation two weeks ago, not much more. I'd like to know if the leak could have come from Camoc, and I want the names of those who've profited from it.'

'Is it the only possible source?'

'No, of course not. There are people in the know in Paris, at the Defence Ministry, and at the SEA, the electronic equipment firm that acts as a cover for the entire operation. But Camoc's name is mentioned in the dossier that's doing the rounds at the moment, whereas in Paris no one's heard of them, apart from the boss of the SEA and myself.'

'Which carrier did you use?'

'Florida Security Airlines.'

'A CIA company. I don't know if that's a security guarantee. But you've always liked to have dealings with the Yanks. Hopeless.'

Bornand closes his eyes and hears Browder, his slightly rasping voice with a strong American accent: 'I'm a friend of your father-in-law, François, we need people like you.' For

Bornand, the meaning was clear: people who were there in Vichy, close to the Germans. After the Liberation, he'd had to keep a low profile, and this felt like a rehabilitation.'

'That's my generation, Jean-Pierre, not yours. I was twenty years old in '45. The Americans came to save us from the Communists, and de Gaulle to boot. I've been working with them since 1947. A leopard doesn't change its spots.'

Moricet shrugs.

'The fact remains that it's still conceivable they could be the source of the leaks. They're also targeting the Iranian market. I wouldn't put it past them to resort to dirty tricks.'

'I don't think so. The CIA's in trouble at the moment. Congress is undergoing a crisis of authority, McFarlane has just been booted off the Security Council. It has absolutely nothing to gain from drawing attention to its own clandestine Iranian arms-dealing networks.'

'Possibly. You're the boss.'

A long silence.

'We need to move fast, Jean-Pierre. I'll take charge of the French side of things. That leaves Camoc. There's no way information on it can be coming out of France.'

'Fine.' Moricet rises, stretches, goes round in a circle and sits down again, his elbows on his knees. 'Fine, I'll go and dig around. The usual rate?'

Sunday 1 December

Noria gingerly pats her police ID in her anorak pocket, like a talisman, and starts her beat at the bottom of rue de Meaux, a street lined with shops between Jaurès and Laumière, no more than a stone's throw from porte de Pantin via avenue Jean-Jaurès, a narrow street where the shops are wedged together. The fine weather's returned, bringing with it a dry, bracing cold. The whole street's in a good mood. She starts off at a greengrocer's, open onto the street, with colourful pyramids of fruit and vegetables reflected in a series of mirrors; the vendors keep up their cheery sales patter and greet their regulars, the customers crowd into the shop stretching the length of the pavement, carrying huge baskets on their arms, taking their time to choose. Today is Sunday.

Noria goes up to the cashier, a plump, faded blonde, hesitates briefly, takes the plunge and shows her police ID:

'Noria Ghozali, police officer.' She smiles to soften the official nature of her visit. 'I don't want to disturb you or take up your time. I just want to show you a photo.'

A kind reception, she's young, this rookie cop. Noria takes out the photo. The woman looks ghastly, the Polaroid doesn't help. Her eyes are closed, she looks in a bad way, but her face is intact, therefore recognisable, and the bullet wound is outside the frame. The cashier calls the staff over, the customers all crowd round, there's a bit of a crush. The answer is unanimous: no, we don't know her.

Noria makes her way up the street going from shop to shop. She has to push through the crowds of customers weighed down with plastic bags, some with buggies. Not many cars around. There's a queue outside the pork butcher's for home-made farmhouse sausages. There's a rotisserie outside the poulterer's, and chickens turn slowly on the spit, huge, sizzling, the fat drops onto the potatoes roasting in the drip pan. The warm air's filled with the smell. Noria slows down. This isn't a Sunday stroll, get a grip. Everywhere, the same reception, welcoming, helpful, a tendency to chat, and the same response: never set eyes on her. The florist, the wine merchant, hardware store, bakeries.

There are still the cafés, four in this little stretch of the street. In the last one, on the corner, with its terrace in the sun, Noria stops for a snack: a hard-boiled egg and a coffee. The customers are all drinking beer, coffee and calvados or white wine.

'Well, have you found your little lady?' asks a fat man in his sixties who's passed her twice in the street, which somehow makes him feel entitled to be familiar.

She smiles.

'Not yet, but I'm getting there.'

'She looks a bit rough in your photo, as if she's on drugs. Why are you looking for her?'

'She's disappeared … '

Noria's tired. Her right ankle's hurting a little, from having walked too much. Her expression is drawn. The owner comes over:

'Aperitif time and it's on me. A glass of white wine, that'll perk you up. You look as if you could do with cheering up.'

Noria hesitates, a fraction of a second: oh to prolong this moment of everyday friendliness, this new-found warm feeling. But it's just not possible. The mere smell of the wine makes her stomach heave. Too bad. She smiles and says: 'No, thank you,' waves a general goodbye and heads off in the direction of avenue Laumière, more shops, more cafés.

Noria feels a sort of conviction. With persistence and method, and that's something she knows all about, she'll find the girl. Today, tomorrow, sooner or later.

Monday 2 December

The weather's grey again, you have to grit your teeth and keep going. On the way to the police headquarters, a detour via the Brasserie des Sports, a stone's throw from the Buttes Chaumont park, a smart area composed of offices and apartment blocks. The Brasserie des Sports is one of those places where the whole neighbourhood drops in at some point or another during the day. To buy cigarettes, have a drink, bet on the horses or purchase a lottery ticket, grab a bite to eat or have lunch with colleagues. It is one of those hubs of neighbourhood life that Noria has pinpointed.

She enters. At this hour, the restaurant is still plunged in semi-darkness. A waiter is laying the tables and there are a few customers leaning on the bar. Noria walks over and orders a hot chocolate and a buttered baguette. The owner is a petite blonde with a frizzy perm, an austere fifty-something, standing behind her till, absorbed in organising the day's work. Noria watches her for a moment then, when the woman looks up, she steps forward, her police ID and the photo of the dead woman in her hand. The owner glances at it:

'Of course I know her, she's one of our regulars. She usually looks better than that. What do you want with her?'

Noria, in a daze, hears herself say:

'She was murdered three days ago.'

Immediately, the news carries the length of the bar. Hubbub. Customers and waiters crowd round. 'She used to come here often ... with a girlfriend, always the same ... Or a male friend who she played snooker with ... do you want to see the snooker table? ... Of course we know her ... Murdered ... Unbelievable ...'

I must work fast and methodically, not get out of my depth, Noria keeps telling herself. Method, method. I can't handle this on my own. Flashback: the police headquarters, the posters, the burden, the loneliness, the chief with his 'be an angel', while she stood there silent and humiliated. Difficult. Flashback, Bonfils: 'My first corpse ... you won't learn much from watching me,' a man who was more approachable.

'I have to call my superiors at the station.'

A quarter of an hour later, Bonfils is there, still laid-back, but now with an air of mild astonishment.

'It's a stroke of luck, pure luck,' says Noria, clutching her card wallet deep in her pocket.

'Of course.' A pause. 'I've just spoken to the superintendent. We have the go-ahead to start taking statements here, he'll inform the Crime Squad. He's quite chuffed to have something to crow about. To work, young lady.'

First of all, the owner. A practical person, she's rummaging through the credit card slips.

'She had lunch here not long ago. Not Saturday or Sunday, on weekends there are fewer people and I'd remember. So Friday? That must be it.' Aloud: 'Who served her? Was it you, Roger? Which table, do you remember? Number 16 ... There you are. Fatima Rashed ...'

A shock. *That name ... Impossible to shake off the feeling that she and I could be distant cousins. Every fibre in me is resisting that kinship. Not with a victim, not with an abandoned corpse.* A glance at Bonfils. *If he dares say a thing, it's war.*

'… Do you want her credit card number?'

Bonfils takes out his notebook and starts to write down the name and number, without saying a word and calls the station again, to have them find her address. Meanwhile, Ghozali sits on the terrace. Friday, the day of the murder. No panic. A steaming hot chocolate, little sips. A completely new feeling, a sort of joy in being alive. Beside her, men are arguing heatedly in a language she doesn't recognise, as they fill in their betting slips.

Bonfils is back. The owner allocates them a round table, not far from the till but slightly set apart so they can question the waiters one by one along with any customers who have something to tell them. Bonfils settles down to take notes and allows Noria, who's taken aback at first, to conduct the interviews. They finish with the barman quickly, his customers are waiting, and besides, she never used to sit at the bar, maybe a tomato juice from time to time, while waiting for a table, not even sure he'd recognise her. But the restaurant waiters are voluble.

'A very beautiful girl, classy, tall, never wore make-up, casual clothes, easy-going.'

'She came regularly, at least twice a week, maybe a bit more often, in the morning at around eleven, to have breakfast – café au lait and scrambled eggs – or lunch between one and two. She'd have the day's special and a coffee. Never a dessert, never any alcohol, never any trouble.'

A waiter hangs a large slate at the entrance to the restaurant. Today's special is Auvergne sausage and mashed potato with Tomme cheese. The regulars arrive. The owner waylays them at the bar and tells them the news, nods towards the cops' table. The restaurant fills up. The atmosphere is friendly, the din grows louder, the waiters move from table to table, weaving around the plants. Noria continues to question Roger:

'Did she come alone, or with someone?'

'Sometimes alone, and sometimes with someone. Always the same two people. A tall girl who looked like a blonde version of her. Or a man, average-looking, hard to describe, not very tall, not very good-looking, thirty-something, maybe a bit older.'

'Have this man or this girl been back since last Friday?'

'No. We haven't seen them.'

'Friday, what time did she come?'

He casts his mind back.

'It's hard to say exactly. I think it was just before the lunch-time rush. Probably earlier than usual. Around twelve, twelve thirty maybe …'

'Was she on her own?'

'No, with the guy. And after lunch, they played snooker, in the basement. They often played. One day, I watched the game, we weren't very busy and I'd finished serving. She played better than him. Much better focus. In my opinion, she was quite an authoritarian woman. I reckon she wore the trousers as they say. But we never saw her arguing with her two friends.'

The restaurant is now packed, the noise level very high. For the cops, it's lunch break. They listen to two elderly pensioners on the next table complaining.

'Nowadays, you try talking to the young about Maxence Van Der Meersch, they haven't a clue who he was. They've barely heard of *L'Empreinte de Dieu,* still less that it won the Goncourt book prize, and even then …'

Noria risks a baffled glance at Bonfils, who smiles at her.

Local office workers are noisily discussing the French hostages being held in Lebanon.

'They've been locked up over there for nearly eight months now. Can you imagine being a prisoner of those raving loonies for that length of time?'

'Didn't you see it all on TV yesterday? The government say they're optimistic, very optimistic …'

'You're kidding … They don't even know where they are, or who's holding them.'

'I'd send in the paras …'

The waiters are rushed off their feet. Precise movements, threading in and out, never empty-handed, and always ready to exchange a few words with one of their customers.

A few regulars pause at the cops' table before leaving. They have nothing to contribute. They often saw Fatima Rashed, but as a matter of fact didn't even know that her name was Fatima. Actually, their paths crossed, that was all. They weren't even able to say what she might have been talking about with her friends.

'When she was on her own, she'd read *Libération*,' says an elderly man in a severe suit disapprovingly.

'So do I,' says Bonfils. 'It's not a good enough reason to go and get murdered.'

The old man remains doubtful.

Two o'clock, and calm is restored. One by one the tables empty. The waiters move less speedily. The owner serves the cops grilled sirloin and chips, apologising that there's no more sausage and mash. An elderly woman comes in to drink a cup of tea. Roger, the waiter who served Fatima Rashed and her friend on the day she was murdered, returns to sit at their table.

'I talked to the boss and she said I should tell you about this. Last Friday, I had the feeling that someone was following Fatima Rashed. I'm not certain, but it came back to me.'

Noria glances at Bonfils, who takes out his notebook without saying a word.

'Tell us anyway, we're interested.'

'The girl and her boyfriend came in and I sat them at table 16.' He points it out in a corner of the restaurant. 'Just behind them, this lone guy I've never seen before walked in. He was wearing a beautiful leather jacket. You know, one of those hip-length jackets, belted at the waist, very fine leather, beautiful. I had the impression it was fur-lined, but I couldn't swear it. I said to myself that a jacket like that would cost me practically a month's salary.' He pauses. 'Without tips, of course. I pointed to the free table next to number 16. There were still quite a few empty tables, which is what makes me think it must have been around midday, you see?' Noria nods to show she follows. 'He said no, and went and sat on the other side of the greenery, as if he didn't want the girl and her friend to see him. Anyway, then I got on with my job – as you've seen, there's no time to hang around. At one point, Fatima and her friend go downstairs to play snooker. They stick around downstairs for forty-five minutes or an hour, as usual.' Bonfils scribbles, makes a quick calculation and whispers to Noria: 'That possibly corroborates the time of the murder.' The waiter goes on: 'I finish clearing the tables, and I go behind the bar for a drink before going home. At the end of the bar, I notice my man with his leather jacket. Fatima and her friend come upstairs at that point and leave. The guy pays for his coffee and sets off in the same direction as them. Perhaps it's just a coincidence.'

'Can you tell us what this guy looked like?'

'Vaguely. Tall, very dark, that French North African type, you know?'

'How old?'

'Around thirty, perhaps a bit older.'

'Would you recognise him?'

'Him, I'm not sure, but the jacket, yes.'

The owner signals to them. 'A telephone call for you.' Bonfils goes to take the call. It's the station. The Crime Squad is on the way to 37–39 avenue Mathurin-Moreau, please meet them in the lobby. She grabs his arm.

'I've been through my bills. It looks as though Fatima's friends paid cash. I can't find any cheques or credit card receipts that match.'

♣

Bornand, ensconced in the executive chair behind his desk, legs outstretched, cigarette dangling from his lips, eyes closed, is letting his thoughts wander. Françoise has gone to stay with a friend – for a break, she said. Without seeing him again. Just a note via Antoine. This woman, who unquestionably belongs to him and always has done, has suddenly escaped his control. She's becoming a vague, disturbing silhouette that disintegrates if he stretches out his hand. A total stranger. And now she's deserting him, leaving him on his own. He feels as if he's suffocating. A whisky.

Enter Fernandez, rested after sleeping round the clock under sedation, at Mado's place. Bornand sits up.

'Listen to this, Fernandez my friend. The unit has informed me of several interesting conversations, and I have some news for you. Chardon's dossier arrived on the desk of the editors of *Combat Présent*, the far-right weekly, this morning. It was a secretary at the *Bavard Impénitent* who thought Bestégui was dragging his feet and decided to take things in hand. If I'm not mistaken, isn't Tardivel, whom we have such a pretty photo of, on the editorial staff at *Combat Présent*?'

'Correct.'

'What do you say to giving him a timely little warning?'

'It'd be a great pleasure, chief.'

'Green light.' A half smile. 'And don't forget to tell me about it.'

'I bumped into Beauchamp on the way in …'

'He was leaving here.'

'You were meeting that right-wing extremist? …'

Fernandez's comment cuts him to the quick. In the past, at the time of the Liberation, the world had been simple: there was the Resistance on one side, collaborators on the other, and he'd been on the wrong side. You had to pretend, beg for resistance certificates, buy them if need be, but, above all else, you had to obtain one. The ultimate humiliation. Once and for all, politics has definitely become a network of personal friendships; the politically correct attitude that the left is left-wing and the right is right-wing – that's pure naivety, and, with age, he is finding it harder and harder to act as if he believes in any of it.

Bornand's face is ashen, his nostrils pinched, as he brings the palm of his hand down hard on the desk.

'You think you're on the left, do you? Look at you. The only things that are on the left are your wristwatch and your gold signet ring. And me? What does the left mean to me, can you tell me? Me, I'm in power, that's all.'

Infuriated, Fernandez bites his tongue.

'As you say, chief. I simply took the liberty of pointing out to you that receiving a veteran of the Organisation de l'Armée Secrète,[6] as close as you can get to a militarised National Front party, here in your office is unwise. If word gets about, it is bound to be misconstrued.'

Bornand rises, turns his back on Fernandez, opens the window, leans out and draws the cold, damp air deep into his lungs. He gazes out over the outline of the rooftops, grey on grey. *Beauchamp is a friend, I've known him for years, we worked together with the Americans. I'm the one who got him a job in the SEA's security department, as soon as I began working with Flandin, and now he's very useful to me. Fair enough, but Fernandez is right, I shouldn't meet him here. Now calm down.* He turns around and says in a neutral voice:

'Mado phoned me an hour ago. Katryn's been murdered ...'

Fernandez sits there, dumbstruck by the news. 'It happened on Friday afternoon, no doubt shortly after you saw her leave with Chardon.'

'Did he kill her?'

'Possibly, I have no idea. In any case, the police are looking for him. Pity, a beautiful and able woman.' Fernandez nods. 'I need you to find out all you can about this Chardon. There's no way he could have obtained that press information by chance, he's got contacts and I'd like to know who they are. He's at the centre of the whole thing, this guy.'

Renewed silence. Bornand sighs.

'And then, this evening, I'm on duty at the Élysée, and that means you are too. Let's plan our evening. You select a few love letters from among the President's correspondence, then phone up and invite them to dinner. Not with the good Lord, but with his saints. As long as it's the Élysée, it'll work.'

'How do you want me to choose them, they don't send photos.'

'No, but we don't give a shit. When we want beautiful girls, we go to Mado's, or to Lentin, the film producer's parties. Model figures guaranteed, and all that goes with it. What I fancy this evening is a surprise, something else, and even, believe it or not, anything. A fat one, for instance, with a double stomach and big, firm breasts, so I can give her a pearl necklace.'

Fernandez sighs.

'I can find you that, but not in the President's postbag.'

♣

The Crime Squad inspectors meet Bonfils and Ghozali outside 37–39 avenue Mathurin-Moreau. Handshakes and a few condescending words of congratulation to the two rookies from the 19th *arrondissement*.

It is a large, modern apartment block, with several flights of stairs. At the centre of this social microcosm is the concierge. She immediately recognises Fatima Rashed in the photo the cops show her, and confirms that she does indeed live there, sharing a flat with Marie-Christine Malinvaud on the ninth floor, staircase D, left-hand door. Two ordinary girls. 'Lived,' say the cops, 'she's been murdered.' Shock. No, she hasn't seen the two girls for a day or two, she couldn't be too sure.

'Could you show us up to their apartment?'

'Of course. I have a key. Just let me lock up my lodge.'

The apartment is empty. The Crime Squad begin a rapid search. Bonfils and Noria stand next to each other on the sidelines.

Inside it is vast, light, quiet. A spacious living room with a terrace running its whole length, a dining area on one side, a lounge area and TV on the other, a few books. Two bedrooms, two bathrooms, a large kitchen. The furniture is comfortable, not particularly tasteful, parquet floors, beige walls. 'A furnished let,' says the concierge.

Women's clothes in the wardrobes, toiletries in the bathrooms, two dirty coffee cups in the sink, a basket of fruit – apples, oranges, bananas, not rotten, the fridge half full, alcohol and soft drinks, supermarket dairy products. A hasty departure perhaps, but no signs of a struggle or violence. In the living room, a large, antique writing desk, full of personal papers. One of the inspectors rapidly leafs through them. Tax returns, bank statements, payslips, rent receipts etc.

'They're both employed by a company called Cominter whose registered office is in Nassau.'

'There's also a garage,' says the concierge. 'They've each got a car. The same make, as a matter of fact. A red Mini for Fatima, a black one for Marie-Christine.'

'Let's go and take a look. We'll come back up afterwards.'

In the underground garage, there's a timer switch affording only a dim light. The concierge points to the double lock-up. The door is simply pushed to. An inspector opens it. Empty. And there, splattered on the right-hand wall at head height, is a dark stain, a long trail down to the ground ending in a dark brown puddle of dried blood. Silence. Noria closes her eyes, overcome. This was where Fatima was shot, her neck split open, the blood on the wall, the body sliding, crumpling, drained. All that remains of the murder are the grisly bloodstains. Bonfils touches her arm. She jumps. Everyone around her has sprung into action.

Two Crime Squad inspectors call the forensic team and

seal off the garage. The others go back up to the apartment to search through the papers, find her flatmate, visit the bank …

Marie-Christine Malinvaud has family in the country, with whom she's still in touch. They phone each other. She's planning to spend Christmas with them in a few days' time. In Pithiviers, the concierge tells them.

Malinvaud, in Pithiviers. Directory inquiries.

An inspector telephones. And finds Marie-Christine.

She's there a few hours later, at Crime Squad HQ, a tall girl with fair hair tied back at the nape with a bow and dull hazel eyes. Wearing baggy trousers, a shapeless anorak and clumpy shoes, she sits wan-faced as she is interviewed by Patriat, the chief of the Crime Squad team investigating the killing of Fatima Rashed. In his grey suit and grey and blue patterned tie, he remains resolutely distant as he conducts the enquiry.

Born in 1963 in Pithiviers. Father a notary's clerk, mother a housewife. No brothers or sisters.

'Yes, we were both part of Mado's call-girl ring, rue de Marignan. Do you know it?' No reply. Half smile. 'You'd be the only ones in the police not to.'

'Let's keep to the point, Mademoiselle Malinvaud. As you know, Fatima Rashed was murdered, and for the moment you're our chief witness. A role you ought to take seriously. Let us resume. How long have you been working for Mado?'

'A year.'

'How did you get into contact with her?'

She shakes her head, her eyes vacant.

'It's such a classic story, that now I can't understand how it could have happened to me. After I left school, I came to Paris to do drama. Actually, I just wanted to get out of Pithiviers.

I enrolled at the Einaudi school and worked part-time in a supermarket to pay for my lessons. I think at that point I still believed in it. People regularly came to watch us work. I started hanging around with Lentin, the film producer, and his crowd. Actors, film technicians, famous people. He promised me small parts in his films as soon as an opportunity came up, and entrusted me to a friend of his, a so-called stills photographer, apparently wanting to put together a portfolio. At that point, I stopped working in the supermarket. He took nude photos of me, I slept with him, and with his friends, telling myself this would help launch my career. He didn't force me, let me make that clear. And then I started with strangers to whom he'd shown the photos and who paid me a lot. I stopped going to drama school, I had no talent to be honest, and I found myself on Mado's books.'

'When did you meet Fatima Rashed?'

'When I arrived at Mado's. She was my mentor, so to speak. And she took her job very seriously. It was she who found us a flat to rent. She supervised my wardrobe, got me to read the novels everyone was talking about, dragged me to various exhibitions, kept an eye on who I was meeting. I think Mado gave her a commission on my clients.'

'And you found it hard to put up with her keeping an eye on you?'

'Not especially. As a matter of fact, I spent several years not thinking for one moment about what I was doing. And besides, Katryn …'

'Katryn?'

'… It's Fatima's *nom de guerre*. And *nom de guerre* it was. I'd say she was a … fascinating woman. She hated men with a single-minded vengeance. The only thing she enjoyed in life was making them pay, and pay as high a price as possible. The idea that a man could touch her without paying would have made her sick, or made her scream. She attempted to pass that hatred on to me, day after day. I don't have that kind of strength, but it was reassuring to see. A sort of call girls' Robin Hood, if you see what I mean?'

'No comment. Why did you run off to Pithiviers the day she was murdered?'

'Katryn was mixed up in a very dangerous game. She was collaborating with a journalist called Chardon. The pair of them entrapped clients and blackmailed them. They weren't Mado's clients, because she's well organised and protected and Katryn would have been busted straight away. But there was a violent incident at Mado's recently, a very young girl who was beaten up by Lentin and his buddies. They'd crossed the yellow line, and I know Katryn intended to make money out of it. The other day, she had a lunch date with Chardon to discuss it.'

'Do you know this Chardon?'

'I've met him several times, that's all, and his story doesn't stack up.'

'Where can we find him?'

'He lives near us, at 38 rue Philippe-Hecht.'

'So, Friday, she was seeing Chardon. And then?'

'We were supposed to be working together in the evening and had arranged to meet back at the apartment at seven. She didn't show up. I went down to the garage to get my car, and I found the wall covered in blood, still fresh, and no Mini. I panicked. I know that Mado's protectors are capable of killing …' She lowers her voice … 'I know that they've already killed … I felt I was in danger because I knew what Katryn was up to. I jumped into my car and drove straight to my parents', without going back up to the apartment.'

'You realise of course that you could have killed Fatima Rashed yourself and that you have a motive for doing so: she was creaming off money from you, in short, and she was spying on you for Mado.'

'Yes, I understand that you see it that way, but I didn't kill her. And I don't think I'm capable of killing anyone.' After a silence: 'I'm afraid, I'm a coward, I'm tired, and I want to change my life. Go back to Pithiviers, marry a pharmacist, have children and play bridge.'

'And why not? You won't be the first prostitute to end up a bourgeois wife.'

Then the group leader turned to his inspectors:

'The priority is to find this Chardon at all costs.'

♣

It's aperitif time in Mado's office. Wearing a simple, well-tailored grey suit, she mixes cocktails with neat, precise movements. She proffers Bornand a stiff whisky sour. He thanks her, and starts taking little sips. Here, he's on well-charted territory, no surprises, no hysterical outbursts, a moment of repose. For Cecchi, her pimp, a tall, well-built man with greased grey hair, the starchy demeanour of a provincial lawyer, but with a heavy, brutal jaw, it's a tequila with a slice of lemon. And for herself, a very light vodka orange.

Cecchi opens the conversation:

'Katryn has been murdered.'

'Mado told me over the telephone.' A long silence. He turns to her. 'Katryn was mixed up with a certain Chardon. I don't know whether you were aware of it?' Mado and Cecchi exchange a glance. 'A gutter press gossip columnist who was prosecuted for living off immoral earnings. That's not good for the reputation of your establishment.'

'I know him,' snaps Cecchi. 'He's always kept well away from Mado's girls, I've made sure of that. How do you know he was mixed up with Katryn?'

'Chardon has a dossier on clandestine arms sales to Iran. No need for me to elaborate further. And he's trying to sell it to the press.'

'Storm warning?'

'Let's say a gale.' Bornand addresses Mado again. 'Last Friday I sent Fernandez to tail Chardon. And he found him having lunch with Katryn in a brasserie near Buttes Chaumont. I have to say I thought she might be his source. I had her working with the Iranians a lot.'

'And was she?'

'No. I've since obtained the dossier. Too well documented. It couldn't have come from Katryn.'

Mado gives Cecchi a questioning look, then says:

'The Crime Squad have heard of this Chardon character. They're looking for him. Apparently he's the last person to have seen Katryn alive.'

'Will you be getting regular updates on the progress of their investigation?'

'I've made arrangements to be kept informed.'

'If you find out anything at all about him, I'm interested. There's no way he could have come across that dossier by chance. I'm looking for any leads that could put me on the trail of the person who gave it to him.'

'Fair's fair, François,' replies Cecchi. 'We don't want Mado's name to appear in the proceedings.'

'I'll take care of that. The prosecutor is a reasonable man and a friend.'

'Excellent.' Mado gets up, and so does Bornand. 'Do you want to try out Katryn's replacement? A novice. You can give her some of your sound advice and tell me what you think. And then have dinner with us.'

'I'm greatly honoured, Mado.' He takes her hand, holds onto it for a moment, leans forward and brushes it with his moustache. She smiles at him. 'But I can't stay. I'm on duty tonight at the Élysée.'

♣

Late afternoon, glorious cool weather over Halat airfield on the road from Beirut to Tripoli. Airfield is too grand a description, more of an air strip, at most two long, broad sections of motorway converted to landing strips, a perfunctory control tower, planes of varying sizes dotted around, hangars sprouting everywhere on the surrounding plain. The hub of all trafficking, controlled by the Christian militia. A pick-up truck laden with sacks rattles its way to Camoc's hangar whose sliding door is wide open, and pulls up inside. The driver and his assistant start unloading the bundles, food products destined for the Lebanese community in Sierra Leone, scheduled to leave tomorrow along with a cargo of arms sent by Camoc. In the midst of the sacks is Moricet. At a signal from the driver, he darts into the hangar and slips behind a stack of wooden pallets. The pick-up drives off. Moricet, lying on his back on the ground, relaxes. *All you need to do is wait, doze off a little. It's going to be a long night.*

Comings and goings inside the hangar, the sacks are brought

over to the plane scheduled to take off tomorrow morning. It's true that it's easier to keep a plane under surveillance than a hangar, and if the Syrians were telling the truth, there's a fair quantity of heroin in among the chickpeas. Gradually, the activity subsides, both inside and outside the hangar, then grinds to a complete halt. Moricet moves over to the door. Beneath his jacket he's wearing a belt full of tools, and in a holster under his arm, his revolver. He breaks open the very rudimentary lock. Half opens the door, looks and listens. It's a clear night, not many lights. Jeeps drive round at regular intervals, but mainly on the runways.

They seem to drive past every half-hour or so. More than enough time.

He has to sprint about a hundred metres across open ground to get to Camoc's offices. He checks his equipment, his gun, emerges from the hangar closing the door behind him, and breaks into a run, doubled over just in case, or out of habit. An almost flat roof, with one pitched side. He jumps, steadies himself, regains his balance, climbs, lies flat. The riskiest part is over. Now to the tools. Using his shears, he makes a hole in the corrugated iron roof, cuts out a square, clears away the insulation materials, slides out the false ceiling, jumps down into the building and replaces the metal square. The alarm is only wired to the doors and windows. He takes a map and an electric torch out of his pocket, gets his bearings and goes straight to the boss's office. All along one wall are metal lockers filled with files. The locks are no problem. It's midnight, and Moricet gets down to work.

Tuesday 3 December

Moricet skims through the various customer files, classified in alphabetical order. He quickly finds confirmation of what the Syrians had told him: large numbers of French and Israeli weapons, fixed up and modified for the Christian militia in Lebanon, the Horn of Africa, with Francophone sub-Saharan Africa the biggest customer, and of course, as it happens, the most interesting. At the centre of the network is the Franco-Lebanese Djimil family. Seven brothers, Shia Muslims, who emigrated in the early 1950s to Côte-d'Ivoire because the Christians controlled all the power in Lebanon. They soon made their fortune. One of them, living in Sierra Leone, organises diamond smuggling, controls virtually half of the country's output, and is now one of the richest men in Africa. A devout Muslim, he finances the works of the entire Shia community in sub-Saharan Africa and maintains close relations with the ayatollahs and the Iranian regime. Another brother, Mohamed Djimil, who stayed in Côte-d'Ivoire, specialises in importing arms. And perhaps also heroin, which often goes hand in hand, but of that, of course, there is no trace in Camoc's correspondence. Huge arms shipments, one average-sized cargo plane a week. Nothing on the ultimate destination, and Camoc only knows Djimil, the middle man. But Moricet has a clear picture of the chain: French mercenaries, African guerrillas, presidential bodyguards and, further afield, South Africa, still under embargo. And of course, Francophone Africa means that there's probably an RPR connection. Besides, it's public knowledge that the Djimil brothers in Côte-d'Ivoire regularly finance the RPR's electoral campaigns. This could be a serious lead. But at the same time, is it really new? It is only confirmation of what had seemed probable from the start. *Anyway, Bornand wants names, I can always give him these, they're credible. Then it's up to him to do what he wants. I've fulfilled my contract. It's two a.m., the airfield is very quiet, may as well carry on ferreting around.*

The next file, a reply from Aurelio Parada, Brazil. Yes, he does have thirty-three toys of superior size and quality, French-made, in working order, from the Argentinean army. *Exocets*, thinks Moricet. *Camoc is ratcheting up its activities.* In the same file, Mohamed Djimil confirms to Camoc that he'll take the thirty-three toys in question, and is immediately transferring the agreed deposit in dollars to Camoc's Swiss bank account. Finally, Parada informs him of the despatch of the toys to the Comores, on 15 November 1985. Moricet feels a rush of excitement. *Comores, Denard, French mercenaries in sub-Saharan Africa, Djimil – you can bet the Exocets will end up in Tehran. The opening up of a new arms supply route to Iran, now that's a valuable piece of information. And Camoc is playing a part in the operation. A political manoeuvre? Bornand can make what he likes of it, not my problem.*

What do I do? Do I take the documents and get out, or do I pick up the boss, as planned? It's four o'clock in the morning. He decides to stay. He crams the files that interest him into a plastic bag, drags a chair over so it will be hidden behind the door when it opens, takes his revolver out of its holster, lays it on his knee, rests his head against the wall, and dozes off.

At eight o'clock, the office slowly comes to life, they're not early risers in these parts. Moricet, concealed behind the door, puts his revolver on the floor. The door opens and a man enters. Moricet kicks the door shut, pinions the man from behind in a stranglehold, tightly enough to prevent him from shouting, and with his free hand gives him an injection in the buttock. In two or three seconds, the body goes limp, Moricet releases his hold and the man crumples to the floor. Moricet checks that it is indeed De Lignières, boss of Camoc, his eyes rolled upwards, his face flaccid. Shoots heroin, according to the Syrians. *As long as he doesn't snuff it straight away.* Moricet puts his revolver back in its holster and from his tool belt he extracts a very large, strong plastic bag and slides the body into it. It's no easy job, the body's limp and heavy and he must move fast. He throws in the files and clamps the bag shut, then goes over to the window, opens it and looks around. Three hundred metres away is his team's little jet, engines throbbing. The only obstacle is exiting the office through the window without being spotted. He has around twenty minutes. He observes the comings and goings for a moment, then lays the bag across the windowsill, jumps out, which costs him a huge effort, and heaves the bag onto his shoulder. The team on board the plane should be ready to intervene if necessary. Nothing happens. Whistling, he heads for the plane. The bag's heavy. No hindrances. He climbs into the plane, throws down the bag and looks at his watch: *ten minutes to go and time to spare.*

Lift-off. De Lignières, propped up in a seat, comes round groggily, in a state of shock. Moricet, leaning against a seat facing him, offers him a bottle of water. De Lignières drinks and splashes his face.

'Let me explain the situation. I work for the SEA, and they're not happy about the disappearance of their plane en route to Tehran.'

The dazed De Lignières appears not to understand.

'The SEA suspects Camoc is involved.'

De Lignières vigorously shakes his head. Impossible.

'Wait. First let me explain the rules of the game. Right now we're circling over Beirut. You answer my questions convincingly and we take you back to Halat, and we don't see each other again. Otherwise ... I take you to Paris, where a reception committee is waiting for you. Shall I begin?'

De Lignières nods.

'The Brazilian Exocets, are they for Iran?'

A shrug.

'I've no idea.' He continues in a completely broken voice: 'I have only one customer, the one who pays. And it's not the Iranians ...'

Moricet leans forward, pressing his finger at a precise point on the sternum. Unable to breathe, a sharp pain shooting up to the back of his neck, De Lignières makes no attempt to defend himself. He's all in.

'Let me put it another way: who are the Djimils working for in this affair? Iran?'

'I think so, but I'm not certain.'

Moricet relaxes the pressure.

'That's better. Explain.'

'We sent a team to Tehran, to take delivery of the SEA consignment. The Iranians asked them to stay to adapt some Exocets due to arrive any day. It can only be those. There aren't that many Exocets circulating freely.'

It all adds up.

'And did you give the Djimils the info on the SEA deliveries to help them eliminate a competitor?'

'That's ridiculous. How do you expect me to? ... I don't

know anything about that delivery. Not the name of the carrier, or the dates, or the airport it left from, nothing … all I know is what's happening in Tehran.'

That also rings true. Moricet straightens up. *I stick my neck out for Bornand, and he sends me up a blind alley. Beirut's my patch, I can't afford to make a mistake. I'll destroy all evidence of my visit to Camoc and give him the Djimils' name. Then he's on his own.* He motions to the two men sitting at the back of the aircraft and goes into the cockpit. The two men bear down on De Lignières, lift him up, one holding each arm, drag him gasping for breath towards the middle of the plane, open the hatch and push him out. Two thousand metres below, the Mediterranean is a violent blue.

♣

The house at 38 rue Philippe-Hecht is locked up, the curtains open, no sign of life. The Crime Squad detectives make door-to-door inquiries around the neighbourhood.

'Of course, everyone knows Chardon, you bump into him all the time, but only to say hello to. You should ask Madame Carvalho, his cleaner, she's a concierge in an apartment block at the bottom of the hill.'

A lively woman, who, no doubt for very personal reasons, does not seem enamoured of the police.

'And besides, up there, we're a community. It's pretty much a family and we don't like people bothering us.' Yes, she cleans for Monsieur Chardon every morning. No, she doesn't know where he is.

'When was the last time you saw him?'

'Friday morning. He was having a bath when I arrived.

Then, he went out for lunch and I finished clearing up. And on Monday, the house was in exactly the same state I'd left it on Friday. Except there was a dirty coffee cup in the sink, which I washed.'

An inspector shows her a photo of Fatima Rashed.

'Have you ever seen this woman?'

'No, never.'

'Could she have come to the house without you seeing her?'

'I'm not up there all the time.'

'This young woman is dead. She was murdered on Friday. And Chardon is the last person to have seen her alive.'

Her expression inscrutable, Madame Carvalho says nothing.

'Could you come to the house with us, while we have a look around?'

'Have you got a warrant?'

'OK, we'll come back tomorrow morning. Eight o'clock outside number 38. Be there to assist with the search. And let us know immediately if Chardon reappears before then. Goodbye, Madame Carvalho.'

The Crime Squad chief drops into the 19th *arrondissement* police headquarters.

'This afternoon, conference in the chambers of the investigating magistrate who's handling this case, at the law courts. She'd like you to be there, Bonfils.'

Then he adds jokingly, as he turns towards Noria:

'We've found the address of Chardon, the man who had lunch with Rashed at the brasserie. He lives around the corner from here, at 38 rue Philippe-Hecht. He seems to have vanished. If you come across him, be a darling and let us know …'

❧

It is twelve forty-five p.m. Tardivel leaves his apartment in the prestigious rue de Marignan, a stone's throw from Mado's place, and walks tranquilly down the street towards avenue Montaigne and place de l'Alma. He has a lunch appointment at Marius and Jeannette's. In his fifties, he has a sinuous, supple body, sparse fair hair, a lifeless face with pointed features, and wears owl spectacles. For the first time in ages, he feels relaxed, the nightmare's over. Chardon, photos, adolescents, blackmail, and, last Saturday, finally, the masters in the post. So yesterday, he dared resume contact with his go-between, an appointment for lunch in a few minutes' time. He's chosen a very good restaurant, near his home, on his expense account, and this evening perhaps … life's looking good again.

On the same side of the street, Fernandez advances in his direction with a buoyant step and a smile on his face, keeping his eyes firmly on the big saloon car with tinted windows driving slowly towards him. When it draws level with Tardivel, Fernandez hastens his step, opens the rear door, shoves him into the car with his shoulder, dives in after him and slams the door. The saloon pulls away without speeding up. No reaction on the pavement, unlike inside the vehicle. Once over the initial shock, Tardivel turns around, tries to open the door, which is locked, and clutches the driver's neck, protesting violently. Then he falls still. The nightmare's back. Rammed right up under his nose, on the back of the driver's seat, is the photo he knows so well of him buggering a very young adolescent, and a kid sitting on the floor, looking despairingly into the lens. Fernandez laughs.

'So, little poofter, calmed down, have we?' Fernandez caresses the back of his neck, the muscles are rigid. 'We've decided to be reasonable, that's better, old fellow.' Tardivel is ashen, slightly bloated, holding his breath, not the slightest defensive movement. 'What about your friends of the "work, family and fatherland" persuasion? A photo like this would cause quite a scandal among your respectable friends, wouldn't it?'

He replies in a hoarse voice:

'I've already paid.'

Fernandez caresses him more intensely.

'I know and I don't give a fuck.'

Moving at a crawl, the saloon turns into place de l'Alma, and onto the freeway hugging the Seine, in the direction of porte de Saint-Cloud.

'Yesterday, your paper received a dossier on the plane that went belly up over Turkey ...'

'I don't know anything about it, I haven't been asked to cover the story.'

Fernandez abruptly tightens his grip on Tardivel's neck making him groan and bangs his head against the door frame; his glasses fly off and Fernandez crushes them underfoot.

'You're going to make damn sure you are asked to cover the story. And take your time to check out the information. All your time. Because the day the story breaks in your rag, I send this photo to your friends, and to mine too while I'm at it.'

Tardivel, his head thumping, dazzling spots of light in front of his eyes, feels himself losing consciousness. Fernandez bangs his head against the door once more.

'For the fun of it,' he says with a real smile. 'Did you hear, faggot? Answer me.'

'I'll do it.'

Fernandez lets him go and looks at his watch. Not even one

o'clock. Enjoyable, but not difficult. He'll have to embroider it a bit to amuse Bornand. He leans towards the driver, whose expression remains deadpan.

'Turn around, we'll drop him off at his lunch appointment.'

'No, drop me here, please.'

'As you wish.'

The car pulls up. Fernandez gets out and holds the door open for him. As Tardivel straightens up, he hits the tip of his chin, half dig, half punch.

'Don't forget me, you filthy little poofter.'

♣

Noria leaves the 19th *arrondissement* police headquarters in the early afternoon. 'Time in lieu,' she announces. Rue Philippe-Hecht, the neighbourhood of the pimping grannies and fire-cracker kids, a godsend.

Madame Aurillac's restaurant is empty at this hour. Sitting alone at a table, she's playing patience and drinking Suze. Very welcoming, Madame Aurillac.

'Sit down and I'll bring you a coffee … the firecrackers stopped after your visit. The kids are still around, of course, making a noise … Monsieur Chardon, rue Philippe-Hecht?' Her face becomes inscrutable. 'No, I don't know him. Never been to the restaurant.'

Noria leaves with the bitter taste of the coffee in her mouth. If you have to choose between a madam and a pimp, which is worse? She walks down the narrow streets. On a long, empty pavement, four kids are taking turns on a skateboard. It's them. Her lucky day. Noria stops and watches them. They're not really expert, but that doesn't stop them showing off. One of the boys picks up the board and walks towards her with a big grin, stopping a couple of paces away.

'Hi, copwoman. What brings you back here?'

The other kids form a circle. Cocky little bastards, like all those she'd hated as a child.

'Hi, Nasser.' The circle closes in. 'I've come to chat to your friend, the restaurant owner.'

Nasser makes an obscene gesture. Noria sits down on a bollard.

'One of her good friends, Chardon, who lives in the brick house over there at number 38, is suspected of murdering a woman, Fatima Rashed ...'

Noria pauses and looks at them. They're listening. A murder has to be worth their attention. On top of that, Fatima Rashed ... They're kids, don't go into detail.

'... Fatima Rashed was my cousin.'

The effect is instantaneous.

'Your cousin? Your family?'

'Exactly. I'm not sure that Chardon's the killer, but I'd like to ask him some questions. He's disappeared. And the restaurant owner knows where he is, but she's refusing to tell me. I was looking for you because perhaps you've seen him in the last few days?'

She glances at the boys. Tacit agreement.

'On Friday, the day it snowed, at around four thirty, five in the afternoon, we were having a snowball fight. The guy was standing at his front door, he was waiting.'

'At number 38?'

'Yes, there. A red Mini came and picked him up ...'

'A Mini?'

'Yes, the soapbox on wheels. He got in next to the guy ...'

'It wasn't a woman at the wheel?'

'No, it was a guy, in a pathetic little car like that. A real sad case.'

Night has fallen. The dark mass of the Buttes Chaumont park broken up by a few haloes of orange light gives off a damp chill. Meanwhile, the nearby rue des Pyrénées is very animated. Noria walks up it slowly, her chest bursting with this new feeling of relaxation, of well-being, alone in the midst of the passing crowds which she scrutinises. There's a second man, it's perhaps … go on, say it, it's probably whoever followed Rashed and Chardon to the Brasserie des Sports. When he picked up Chardon, Rashed was most likely already dead. An accomplice of Chardon's? Rashed's killer? The killer of both? There's a second man, and I'm the only one who knows. She's in no hurry to go home.

The bus shelter affords a pocket of light. Noria stops in her tracks. Facing her is a poster depicting a man, larger than life, full-frontal and bare-chested, perched on the edge of a piece of furniture, black and white underpants, tight and bulging, his face slightly fuzzy, his profile turned to the left, his eyes lowered, vaguely absent, submissive, offering himself. *Bonfils.* A total shock. She hesitates and is unable to tear her eyes away. She lets herself go, with pleasure. The sharply contrasting black and white photo is magnificent. His chest and stomach muscles are rippling, well-defined, alive. She wants to trace the contours with her finger, stroke the smooth skin. Attractive, the groin, just hinted at. A hot flush, the shock. She presses her palms on the glass, over his nipples, leaving two moist patches. The three women waiting for the bus watch her in amazement. Noria smiles at them and goes on her way. She pictures Bonfils, cigarette dangling from his lips, 'You won't learn much from watching me.' *That depends.*

❦

Bonfils and the Crime Squad meet at the Brasserie des Deux Palais before going up to the office of Magistrate Luccioni who is in charge of the investigation into Fatima Rashed's murder. 'Not exactly a pushover,' says the group leader. Then, corridors, staircases, followed by a door into a cramped, ill-lit office. They are greeted by a tall, very slim, almost skinny, woman with a striking, angular face; big, very pale greenish-blue eyes, a prominent nose, high cheekbones, dark hair cut just below the ear. She's wearing a silk shirt and a flowing grey mid-calf-length skirt, slit down one side, which makes her look even taller. She conspicuously glances at her watch.

'I was waiting for you, gentlemen.' She indicates three chairs. 'Take a seat.'

She skilfully cultivates a frosty image and smells of mint, thinks Bonfils, suddenly interested.

The Fatima Rashed dossier lies open on her desk. The group leader goes over the young woman's civil status: born in Algiers in 1958, obtains a three-month tourist visa for France in 1978, and arrives alone. And stays. Meanwhile the magistrate ticks off the details in the dossier. Situation regularised in 1980, granted French citizenship in 1983.

The magistrate looks up:

'The authorities don't always move so fast. I assume her case was fast-tracked …'

'That is possible.'

'Just in case, try and find out by whom. Go on.'

'Fatima Rashed was single and lived at 37–39 avenue Mathurin-Moreau, in the 19th *arrondissement*. Murdered in her garage on 29 November, between 14.00 and 17.00 hours, by a single shot to the throat. The bullet exited through the back of her neck, making death instantaneous. The bullet has been found and is currently being examined by the forensic team.'

'I see that it was a 357 magnum cartridge. Isn't that a calibre used by the French police?'

'It is. But it's a fairly common calibre.' A pause. 'The murder took place during a struggle, apparently. The victim had wounds to her fingers and the palms of her hands, a large bruise on her right arm and had probably bitten her attacker.' The magistrate makes notes in the margins. 'The body was then dumped in the Zénith open-air parking lot at La Villette. Yesterday we found and questioned the young woman who was Rashed's flatmate, Marie-Christine Malinvaud at the Vice Squad headquarters on the quai des Orfèvres. She states they were both employed as part of Mado's call-girl ring.'

'Which would explain the payslips from Cominter?'

'Exactly. We've checked her bank account and she made regular deposits corresponding to the amounts on the payslips.'

'Can we locate this company?'

'I doubt it. Its registered address is in the Bahamas.' A pause. 'Neither Malinvaud nor Rashed have a record with the Vice ...'

'Knowing the Vice, that's no surprise.'

A frosty silence.

'Shall I go on?' She motions him to continue. 'Still according to her flatmate, Rashed was apparently involved in blackmailing operations with a journalist called Chardon. Chardon was sentenced to two years in 1980 for living off immoral earnings, and he does indeed seem to have been mixed up in various attempts to blackmail well-known personalities and politicians, and our colleagues in Intelligence have told us that they sometimes use him as a paid informer.'

'That last point isn't mentioned in the dossier.'

'As a precaution, your honour.'

'Who are you suspicious of, inspector? Of me? Of magistrates in general? I shall make a point of noting in the dossier that Chardon is in the pay of the Intelligence Service.'

The group leader sighs and continues:

'We visited Chardon's residence this morning. It seems he left on the day of the murder and hasn't returned since. Furthermore, we showed photos of him to the witnesses, and he was definitely the person who had lunch with Rashed on the day of the murder. We are questioning neighbours, we're looking for his family, possibly also for a car ... We've made no progress. As far as we're concerned, Chardon is the main witness, if not the prime suspect. And we plan to carry out a search of his home and make inquiries at the various newspapers he's written for.'

'Fine, I'll grant you a search warrant. Tell me, I see from the case file that, according to Malinvaud's statement, a very young girl was attacked at Mado's, and that this could have something to do with the murder. Do you have any suggestions as to how to tackle this aspect of the case?'

'No, your honour, not for the time being.'

'To sum up. Rashed and Chardon, pursue the leads you've already mentioned. As regards Cominter, I'll talk to the Fraud Squad. By the way, I contacted Madeleine Prévost, known as Mado, and asked to interview her as a witness in the Fatima Rashed murder case.' She allows a silence to hover. 'Do you have a file on her?'

The group leader finally ventures a reply:

'We all know Mado, your honour. Several superintendents, including some of the best-known of them, are regulars of hers. She's in the pay of the Vice and the Intelligence Service, subsidised by the Ministry of Foreign Affairs. She's protected by the entire political elite, both left and right. Mado has been a republican institution for the past fifteen years. She'll be awarded the Legion of Honour ahead of me.'

'I see. She told me she had nothing to do with this business, nothing to say in general, and in particular, nothing to say to magistrates under any circumstances. Do those on the payroll of the Intelligence Service normally behave like this towards magistrates?'

'In a manner of speaking ... That's what's going to complicate this case.'

'A prostitute and a pimp protected by the police; a suspect who's in the pay of the Intelligence Service; a murder committed with a weapon that might be a service weapon ... don't you find, inspector, that this case is likely to turn into a can of worms?'

The group leader (*bitch, you think I don't know it*) sits stony-faced saying nothing. Bonfils is enjoying the situation. The magistrate concludes:

'I'll deal with Madeleine Prévost.'

Then she turns to Bonfils and smiles at him, a magnificent smile. Her face is transformed, the harsh features soften, her full lips are fleshy and beautiful. A sensual woman beneath the ice. Bonfils gets a hard-on.

'I asked you to come because I wanted to thank you personally for your contribution to the investigation. Outstanding, your identification of the victim.'

Outstanding, yes, but not thanks to me. And I'm not going to tell her. He returns her smile.

'Thank you.'

The cops cross the boulevard and go for a drink at the Brasserie des Deux Palais, talking of this and that, but carefully avoiding the subject of the case conference that has just taken place. The group leader is keeping his remarks for his squad. Bonfils already feels as if he's elsewhere, back in the 19th *arrondissement*, which doesn't exactly fill him with joy. A few minutes later, on the other side of the road, the magistrate leaves the courts and heads towards the Latin Quarter.

'If she goes for Mado, she won't survive,' says the group leader.

Bonfils pays for his drink, says goodbye and leaves. Walking quickly, he catches up with the magistrate on pont Saint-Michel. She walks very erect, taking large strides. Her severely-tailored black ankle-length overcoat flaps rhythmically against her boots. Around her neck, a thick white woollen scarf hides the lower part of her face. She's bareheaded, completely withdrawn from everything going on around her: passers-by, cars, traffic jams. Bonfils adjusts his pace to match hers, mesmerised by the swaying of her hips, as regular and precise as a metronome. She continues up boulevard Saint-Michel, on the right-hand side, which is less crowded. Bonfils allows himself to be swept along, half for the fun of it and half spurred on by desire. She keeps close to the forbidding grey walls of the Lycée Saint-Louis – the colour suits her – still at a rapid pace. The boulevard climbs uphill. Bonfils imagines the moistness of her neck underneath the scarf as he fantasises about breaking through the frosty gaze, running his hands through her damp hair and sparking that radiant smile. She turns right, alongside the Jardin du Luxembourg, empty at this hour, in the teeth of the icy wind. Bonfils allows her to put a distance between them. She crosses rue d'Assas and goes into the lobby of a very modern apartment block, built entirely of glass. Standing across the street, he sees her profile as she takes her mail from her letter box, then she turns her back to him, calls the lift, waits and disappears. He goes into the building. She's gone up to the eighth floor. He inhales a vague fragrance of lime and fresh mint, which evaporates. That was it.

Wednesday 4 December

The Crime Squad is outside Chardon's house at eight a.m., the concierge as wary as ever. No, she hasn't seen him. She opens the door. The house, immaculately neat and tidy, feels as though no one is living there. The cops hesitate briefly in the hall, then one group attacks the ground floor, garage, junk room and darkroom, while the other begins with the bedroom on the second floor, escorted by the concierge.

It has a blue fitted carpet, and a double bed with a blue and white Sicilian bedspread. The cops pull the covers off the bed, shake the sheets and pillows and turn the mattress over. There's no indication that it has been opened up or tampered with. The concierge bustles about tidying up after them.

A wall is taken up by cupboards: clothes, no obvious gaps, casual, expensive clothes, nothing else. In the pocket of a pair of velvet trousers they find a white sheet of paper folded into four bearing the letterhead of a company, the SEA, electronic equipment, covered in a jumble of figures and operations. In a corner of the page, two lines have been circled: Bob-750 and underneath: C-200. C: Chardon perhaps? They remove it.

There are some books on a low shelf, a few Gérard de Villiers and two John Le Carré novels, travel books and memoirs on Africa, and a huge history of South Africa. Around thirty altogether, nothing concealed between the pages. There's also a small television and radio. The wall is covered with a splendid collection of African masks. No photos, no letters, no women's underwear, no personal items.

'Strange bedroom. Rather tame for a pimp.'

The concierge is scandalised.

They move into the white-tiled en suite bathroom. Hygienic. Classy but not extravagant toiletries. Liquid soap, bath foam, men's eau de toilette, aftershave, all poured down the washbasin, nothing out of the ordinary there. Electric shaver, a lone toothbrush. In a little cabinet are some everyday medicines, some of them past their expiry date. A dressing gown and pyjamas hang on the back of the door.

'A real stay-at-home boy, our customer. This is getting bloody boring.'

Then the office. Now that's more interesting. An inlaid Louis XV writing desk. 'A beautiful piece of furniture,' comments one of the cops, opening the lid. On the right are a few handwritten sheets, which they remove. On the left there are bills and credit card receipts in cardboard folders: clothes, food, and a 60,000-franc item of jewellery from Cartier's. Maybe the pearl Fatima Rashed was wearing when she was killed? To be checked. Bank statements. Books of stamps, envelopes, a drawer full of felt-tips, ballpoint pens, a Montblanc fountain pen, a bottle of ink. A diary that does not appear to belong to him, and a set of keys that are not the keys to his place. The cops take them. And a personal accounts book showing payments for the various freelance newspaper articles he's written.

'Completely up to date,' comments a cop.

He points at one entry. The SPIL, which publishes the *Bavard Impénitent*. He leafs through the pile. *A regular informer, as well. That's amusing. A rag that's always on our backs. We'll make sure this gets out. In the meantime, we'll take it.*

Next to the writing desk is a photocopier. Switch it on. It works, and the paper tray is full. On a table by the window is a typewriter, neatly put away, a telephone, and an address book. They take that too.

The first-floor living room. No furniture, so that doesn't take long. And the kitchen: cupboards, food, pots and pans, a rubbish bin, nothing to attract attention.

They meet up in the hall. The haul: a few papers that need to be studied in more detail, but nothing earth-shattering by the looks of it. The darkroom is empty and clean. Of course, his archives are kept somewhere safe. Where? To be investigated further. The downstairs toilet door is open. Clean, with a very ancient flush, a cast-iron cistern high on the wall.

'I haven't seen one of those for years,' says an inspector. 'When I was a kid, we had a flush like that and my mother put dried cod in there to soak ...'

He clambers onto the seat and runs his hand around the cistern, feels an object and fishes out a package carefully wrapped in sheets of plastic. He places it on the table in the darkroom, the cops gathered round in a circle. A clean incision, tastes it on the tip of a knife: heroin.

'Does that change the picture?'

'Not necessarily.'

But it radically changes the concierge's opinion of Chardon.

♣

Fernandez enters the bar at Mado's with a heavy heart. Cecchi has summoned him. He's over there, Cecchi, at the back, waiting for him at a low coffee table, affecting to look relaxed. He's with his driver and a bodyguard, both of them burly, in dark suits, and frankly, that doesn't bode well. Their presence suggests a lynching rather than negotiation. Fernandez sits down and Cecchi orders whiskies all round. Then he gets straight to the point:

'There was a search right here this morning, of the whole place. That goes against our agreement.'

'Bornand's dealt with it. Proceedings to remove the magistrate who ordered the search will begin this afternoon.'

Cecchi sighs. 'That'll be better for everyone. Let's change the subject.' Fernandez waits. 'You killed Katryn, my dear friend Fernandez. And she's one of my girls.' Fernandez, sinking into the banquette, his throat tight, unable to utter a word, stares at Cecchi. 'Your boss can't keep you in line. Cocaine will be your undoing. If you start messing with coke again while you work for me, you'll wish you'd never been born.'

Coke, the party at Mado's, the naked woman with black hair, and then a complete blank. Cecchi goes on:

'The other evening, you were out of it. Mado didn't have to use any pressure to get you to tell her everything. We can easily put the Crime Squad on your trail, or inform Bornand.'

Mounting nausea, the garage, the girl screaming, her neck split open, going round and round in his mind to the pounding of his heart. Cecchi leans towards him:

'You belong to me now. Do you understand? Answer me.'

I'm no longer in control. I'm running to stand still. Alone. The police intelligence service, all cops together, a lost paradise.

'It looks like it.'

'Sensible, that's good. What's happened to Chardon?'

Is this a trap? Think fast, keep a grip. He can't really know anything, keep to damage limitation and we'll see later.

'I have no idea. He and Katryn had lunch in a brasserie

in the 19th *arrondissement*, they parted company, I followed Katryn.' He pauses. 'Bornand thought she might be Chardon's source.' Cecchi nods. 'I threatened her, to frighten her, she struggled and the gun went off.'

Cecchi ponders for a few moments. It seems to stack up. When the police find Chardon, he'll be the first to know, and then they'll see where they stand. Meanwhile, he's not going to waste tears over a girl he'd have had to bust anyway, since she was working with Chardon. Which seems pretty certain.

'Let's talk business. I want to obtain authorisation to reopen the Bois de Boulogne gambling club. And fast. Before the March election, because your Socialist friends are going to lose and we'll all be back at square one.'

'Bornand doesn't have any friends or contacts in the Interior Ministry.'

'I'm counting on you to help him make some. This dossier that he's so afraid of, do you know what's in it?'

'Yes, I've read it. The sale of missiles to Iran. All entirely clan- destine. He brokered the deal, but his name isn't mentioned anywhere. It may be careless, but I don't see that it represents any serious danger for him.'

'Can you get hold of this dossier for me?'

'That's difficult. But it's reached the editors of *Combat Présent*.'

'Then I'll take care of it. For the rest, you have carte blanche, you know Bornand and his tricks better than I do. And I expect results.'

Heard that somewhere before.

'I'll find a way.'

'You have no choice.'

Fernandez, his hands folded between his knees, glances at

the two motionless bodyguards, their expressions blank. *Not this, not this life.* At the sight of his disgruntled face, Cecchi laughs:

'There isn't only the stick, there's also the carrot. If I receive the permit, I'll wipe out your debt, and I'll bring you into the casino with me. The way things are right now, it's a safer bet than the Élysée, believe me.'

Thursday 5 December

Bornand reaches Lamorlaye before seven a.m. and parks near the training track. Before even seeing the horses, he can hear them galloping behind the curtain of trees, a dull, irregular thudding that reverberates deep in his chest, in waves, at regular intervals. He switches off the engine of his Porsche. Windows wound down, eyes closed, he listens with a lump in his throat. No going back now ... All that matters is the rhythm of the galloping, in sync with his heartbeat. A foretaste of the race. There's nothing comparable to the thrill he experiences in the last hundred metres with the riders at full pelt, when he sees his horse put on a final spurt, inch by inch forge into the lead and push its muzzle over the finishing line first. A feeling that he's bursting inside, an apocalyptic state of bliss. Bornand remembers having cried the first time one of his colts won. Coming second is nothing less than a calamity.

He collects himself, slips a pair of wellington boots over his town trousers, puts on a fur-lined jacket and walks through the woods to the Aigles racetrack. He emerges in a sandy clearing where four horses are walking round in step, ridden by helmeted stable lads. Long strides, necks straining, taut, elongated muscles under their gleaming coats, beautiful to behold. Elegant. All four of them. And so alike they could be siblings. Bornand immediately spots his colt Crystal Palace, a burnished bay, up front, stepping with exquisite grace. He has a precise recollection of every racehorse he's owned. The colour of their coat, their markings, their style, their idiosyncrasies, and the course taken by every race he's ever attended, down to the last detail. Four men are talking together at the centre of the clearing: the two jockeys who'll be riding the horses in the race, the trainer and Karim, his partner at the International Bank of Lebanon for more than ten years. A complete surprise. A nasty surprise: Bornand has a feeling Karim has come to talk business and ruin his day. *Don't give anything away.* Handshakes all round.

'We were waiting for you,' says the trainer. 'Let me put you in the picture. The two three-year-olds are running in the fifteen hundred metres. The grey will lead them to the start, gently, at a walk, the chestnut will act as pacesetter at the start of the race.' To the jockeys: 'At thirteen hundred metres, give them their head. It's the last two hundred metres I'm interested in.'

The jockeys replace the stable lads on the two colts, and, following the line of trees, the group heads towards the starting line at the far end of the wide, tree-fringed, slightly undulating turf track. The two men gaze after the receding horses; they disturb two hinds which take fright and bound across the track. Karim's presence irritates Bornand, it's like having a stone in one's shoe.

'What are you doing here, Karim?'

'Pretty much the same as you. I've got a colt competing.'

'And you've come from Beirut for the training?'

'I was in Paris. I found out you'd be here this morning, and I grabbed the chance to see you. I wasn't able to get hold of you on the phone yesterday.'

'What do you have to talk to me about that's so urgent?'

'Are you kidding?'

'Not at all.'

'You recall that the IBL is implicated in the arms delivery to Iran that just ballsed up? The bank's covering the operation …'

Bornand finds it hard to breathe, feels the blood drain from his face. He concentrates on the horses now on the track. They're off. Concealed in the dip, you hear them before they come into view, and the pounding of their hooves heralds the magic moment when they reappear. They come charging down, all three flank to flank, their breath sounds as if drawn from deep within them. Bunched together on the flat, they gather speed, draw level with the watching men, the brown bay a head in front of the others. A thrilling moment. At the end of the track, the jockeys straighten up, bring the horses to a halt, and slow down to a walk.

'Well, the chestnut put on a spurt at the end.'

'She was pushed to the limit, whereas Crystal managed it easily.'

No one said a word about Karim's colt which was trailing behind. Not at all ready. A pretext of a race, clearly. Bornand has regained his composure.

Back to the ring, where the horses are walking in step, their heads down, dripping with sweat, their veins bulging, steaming, snorting. The stable lads unsaddle them and rub them down. Bornand borrows a damp cloth to clean out Crystal's nostrils.

The trainer walks a few paces with the jockeys and the owners.

'In the race, try and keep Crystal's blinkers on pretty much until the home straight, I leave that up to your judgement. He's always been a front runner, but that'll have to change if we want him to race longer distances. He proved this morning that he can pull it off at the last lap.'

The jockey nods. Turning to Bornand:

'Crystal Palace is in with a real chance on Sunday.'

'I won't be able to watch him race, I'll be out of the country.'
The jockey nods again. The trainer turns to Bornand:

'Call me after eight p.m.'

The lads lead the horses back to the stables, the trainer and
the jockeys follow them, the woods are deserted. Karim and
Bornand are left alone. Bornand picks up where they left off:

'The bank didn't invest a cent in the operation, and therefore hasn't lost anything.'

Karim replies: 'Which isn't the case as far as you're concerned. The Iranians have already cashed your guarantee of a
million dollars …'

'I took the risk. After all, I'm not exactly out on the street
yet. And from what I've heard, you lost similar sums at the
Beirut casino, in the good old days.'

Laughter.

'Gambling and business aren't the same thing at all. Losing
at cards is still enjoyable. Losing in business … But seriously,
you were reckless, you were too greedy, you'd have done better
to work through our usual brokers.'

'Are you lecturing me?'

'It's not a question of lecturing, but of risk management.
First of all, by cutting them out, you upset the traditional
Middle East arms brokers. They're powerful people, and our
best customers. I hope you're not forgetting that …'

'I'm not forgetting it …'

'And besides, if there's a scandal in France …'

'There won't be a scandal. I've identified the people behind the
attack and the press dossier. They're also involved in arms deals
with Iran. I went to meet them yesterday in their stronghold.'

He falters. 'In Côte-d'Ivoire. I can ruin them and they can ruin me. So we came to an understanding. They cut it out and everybody minds their own business. The incident is closed.'

'I beg to disagree. First of all because you may be wrong as to who's behind the operation, there are a number of interests at stake. And secondly because French political life is a sack of cats nowadays, and the scandal can be re-ignited from just about any quarter. So, to continue. If there's a scandal, there'll be an inquiry. And if there's an inquiry, you'll be in the eye of the cyclone. A bank like the IBL needs absolute calm and discretion to function properly.'

'What are you suggesting?'

'It must be made impossible to trace things back to the IBL via you. Close all your accounts. Use cash, that's always the best way to cut all connections. And I'll erase all trace of the accounts.'

Bornand holds his tongue, looking down at his boots sinking into the thick, sodden turf. The bitter taste of friendship betrayed. The house surrounded by flowers looking down over Beirut, full of fragrances so much warmer than here in France, the beautiful Syrian woman I gave him, and his first horse which I chose for him. Flashback to the stands at the Beirut racecourse, with its walls riddled with machine-gun rounds, the shooting that stops just long enough for the race to take place, Karim winning, the two men embracing at the finishing post … Karim continues:

'I've already made arrangements with our Geneva correspondent. They're expecting you.'

Chilled to the bone, Bornand shivers. *Think fast. So this is what it's come to. Business is business. It's him or me. Time to take advantage of the circumstances to cover my tracks.*

'I'll send someone next week.'

Before driving back to Paris, Bornand stops for a coffee and brandy at the bar-cum-tobacconist's in Lamorlaye and reads *Paris Turf*.

♣

'Fernandez? Cecchi here.' Fernandez has recognised him – his master's voice. 'I've got some news on Chardon. Bornand won't be disappointed. First of all, he served in the Marines for five years, in Gabon and Côte-d'Ivoire, from 1973 to 1979. I'm not sure that's relevant to our particular business, but just in case … Then he resurfaces on the payroll of the Intelligence Service. You didn't know that?'

'No.' *What an arsehole. That record, so bare, of course. I'm losing my touch.* 'You'll have to do a bit better than this in future. And finally, the cops found around a hundred grams of heroin at his place, Lebanese. He doesn't seem to be a junkie, so he's a dealer, small time at any rate. The Crime Squad's done well, in two days. That'll give Bornand something to mull over. Remind him that I never do favours for free.'

Cloistered in his Élysée office, Bornand doodles feverishly, drawing acanthus leaves on his notepad. Last night he spent an hour in a *tête-à-tête* meeting with the President, who as usual didn't want to hear about arms sales, but noted the fact that the current problem was resolved, and seemed satisfied. He draws another line, rips out the page, crumples it into a ball and bins it. Fernandez, sitting opposite him, waits.

'So, where are we up to with Tardivel?'

'Mission accomplished. Raymond, an old friend from

Intelligence, and I abducted the little faggot in the middle of the street, not far from here. No one batted an eyelid. As soon as he saw the photo, he caved in. I beat him up a bit, not badly.' Flashback, squeezing the back of his neck, which yielded, submissive. He smiles. 'More for pleasure than from necessity, to be totally frank. There won't be any more talk of the Chardon dossier from that quarter.'

Bornand does not react. Fernandez continues:

'Chardon was blackmailing him all right, and Tardivel paid up. But that's not all. I had a call from Cecchi this morning. The investigation is progressing. The cops have established that Chardon is an ex-Marine and was stationed in Gabon, and they found a little stash of Lebanese heroin at his place ...'

Bornand's ears suddenly prick up. Chardon encounters the Djimil brothers while he's serving in Africa, stays in touch trafficking Lebanese with them, and they use him to take their dossier to Paris. The piece fits into the jigsaw.

'... Again according to Cecchi, Chardon is in the pay of the Intelligence Service.'

Bornand is gutted. He leans back in his chair, his eyes closed, his breath coming in short convulsive gasps, his face ashen, his hands clasped. For several minutes. Fernandez starts getting worried. *Heart attack?* Then Bornand's muscles gradually relax, his breathing returns to normal, he remains motionless for a while longer, before opening his eyes and sitting up.

'That changes the whole picture. Pay attention to what I'm saying. The Djimils plan the job with Chardon, who informs the Intelligence Service, his paymaster. Intelligence leap at the opportunity and kill two birds with one stone. They give us a completely abridged dossier on Chardon ...'

'That's how they always protect their informers.'

Bornand bangs his fist on the desk.

'Shut up, Fernandez. It's common knowledge that the police department is at war with the Élysée unit. And the unit is Grossouvre, Ménage and myself. So if Intelligence have been informed of this business by Chardon, they'll have no hesitation in using it to bring me down and cripple the Socialists in the March elections too while they're at it.' In a sudden outburst of rage, his voice quavering, he continues: 'This just proves they're a bunch of uncontrollable incompetents. Don't tell me any different.'

'I haven't said a word, sir.'

Bornand gets up and turns to the window. The roofs look bare. He takes two deep breaths and tries to regain his composure. A bad day. The pleasure of the horses ruined this morning, being ditched by a friend, and now the whole business has become more complicated, just when he thought he had things under control. He speaks without looking at Fernandez.

'Who's behind Chardon? Your old boss Macquart? We have to seize the initiative. I'm going to warn the unit. We'll see what blocks to put in place, we'll find a chink. They're not invulnerable, these Intelligence cops, are they, Fernandez? They have their little vices, their little weaknesses, like you, like everyone else ...'

Fernandez pictures Macquart, forthright, massive, behind his desk, a cop to the very marrow. He lives in the countryside under a false name; nobody knows his family; he always checks that he's not being followed when he leaves the office; all the more upright because he's not interested in money. The chink ... Bornand's going to come a cropper, and he knows it, and Fernandez rejoices.

'... Then I'll go and see the Interior Minister to have a word with him about the way some of his departments operate.' He turns around. 'Disbanding the Intelligence Service was in his electoral manifesto in '81, wasn't it, unless I am much mistaken?'

'It was more or less in the manifesto.'

'Well I think it's time to remind him.'

'Sir, if you see the Minister, you know that Cecchi is waiting for his authorisation to reopen the Bois de Boulogne gambling club, which Intelligence is blocking.'

Surprised, Bornand stares at him and thinks for a moment.

'I don't think it's appropriate to confuse the two issues.'

'Cecchi is very useful to you, especially at the moment ...'

'Cecchi seems to me to be rather too compromising an individual under the circumstances. And I've got him on-side, in any case. I'll look into that later, when I have the time and more elbow room.' A silence. 'Intelligence must have sent Chardon to a safe house. We're not likely to see him again.'

'That's for sure.'

♣

Back at the police station, a crushing workload has accumulated over the past few days. Noria and Bonfils plod on in silence. Noria looks up from time to time and glances at Bonfils, who doesn't react, seemingly absorbed in his tasks.

Lunch break. After a dull morning, it's now a glorious day. Bonfils suggests having a sandwich on a bench out in the sunshine, in the Buttes Chaumont park overlooking the lake. It's still cold, but it makes a change from the office. He sits there, legs outstretched, silent, half absent. He finishes his sandwich under Noria's gaze. A clear-cut profile, lips parted, very well defined. His jacket is open. Under his grey polo-neck sweater, she can make out his regular breathing beneath the bulge of his chest. She has a clear image in her mind of the photo and wants to slip her hand under the wool and touch his skin, and let it linger there, with his nipple in the hollow of her palm. It's fun toying with desire and ambiguity. These are completely new feelings for her. Halt there.

'You didn't come in to work yesterday?' she said.

'I took a day off. I was feeling down.'

'I've got news of Chardon.'

Bonfils suddenly sits up.

'You never give up …'

She wants to tell him about running away, the loneliness. But the words simply won't come out.

'Should I?' she queries.

'To be honest, I don't know.'

And now she's aggressive:

'Well I don't have a choice.'

He gazes at her for a moment in silence, then says:

'If you say so. Shoot.'

'Chardon went home after leaving the Brasserie des Sports. He went out again alone at around four thirty, and a man driving Fatima Rashed's Mini came and picked him up outside his house. He got into the car and hasn't been seen since.'

'How do you know that?'

She tells him about the house, the day it snowed, the kids in the street and their snowball fight … Bonfils looks pensive.

'By that time, it's likely that Rashed was already dead.'

'The driver is almost certainly the man who followed him to the restaurant. Perhaps he and Chardon are accomplices.'

'This is exciting. We should go back to the brasserie and try to find out more about this guy, and file an additional report. We'll take it to the investigating magistrate.'

'To the magistrate? Why not to the Crime Squad?'

He has dimples when he smiles.

'Because the magistrate is a lot more attractive than the section boss at the Crime Squad.'

The irony is not lost on Noria: *If you find him, be a darling and let us know ...*

'OK, we'll give it to the magistrate.'

Friday 6 December

At nine a.m. Bonfils and Noria turn up at the law courts. There's no time to lose, at the station the pressure's on. The clerk is alone in the office, sitting at her typewriter, and clearly surprised to see them.

'Haven't you heard? Proceedings have begun to remove the magistrate from the case.' They are open-mouthed. 'On Wednesday morning she went to search Madeleine Prévost's premises, and I went with her, naturally. She didn't call in the Crime Squad because she was afraid there might be a leak. So she asked the chief of the 8th *arrondissement* to provide her with police backup. And on Wednesday evening, the public prosecutor informed her that he was referring the case to the Court of Criminal Appeal because she had overstepped her prerogative.'

Bonfils has difficulty in maintaining his composure. Flashback: *'If she goes for Mado, she won't survive.'* She hadn't survived. The clerk continues:

'On Wednesday evening, she left feeling very shaken, and there's been no sign of life since. I phone, no answer. It's odd, because her mother lives with her and she never leaves the apartment these days.'

As they leave the courts, Bonfils takes Noria's arm.

'We're going to the magistrate's place to make sure nothing's happened to her. It's not far, only about fifteen minutes' walk.'

Noria pulls up her anorak collar. *Utterly disconcerting, this*

guy. He finds the magistrate attractive. He knows where she lives.
Is he sleeping with her? What's he dragging me into? But curiosity
gets the better of her.

They walk up to the jardin du Luxembourg and turn into rue
d'Assas, Bonfils tense and slightly distant. A grey light over the
gardens, a flat prospect with a few rare visitors strolling up and
down. On reaching rue d'Assas, Bonfils heads for a modern
apartment block, built entirely of glass, enters the lobby and
walks over to the lift – with the assurance of someone who is
familiar with the building. Noria follows him. On the eighth
floor, he rings the bell insistently. There's no response. Bonfils
goes to fetch the concierge, who follows him up with a set of
keys and opens the door. Three locks, one after the other. They
go in, call out, silence. To the left is a vast living room with
two huge French windows that open onto a veranda protected
by a metal grille. Empty. To the right, a kitchen, empty. Facing
them, a corridor. First bedroom on the right, empty. Second
bedroom, an elderly woman lying peacefully on a bed, her
arms by her sides, wearing a well-tailored navy-blue suit. They
approach the bed. Bonfils touches the emaciated, deeply jaun-
diced face with the back of his hand. It is stone cold: *of course,*
she's dead. The concierge invokes God almighty and groans.
Noria stops breathing, her breath trapped in her chest, knowing
the worst is certain. At the end of the corridor is the bathroom
door. Bonfils opens it, reels and rushes into the kitchen. Noria
leans forward and peers through the open door. In the bathtub
is a naked woman, her head slumped onto her chest, her face
concealed by a mop of short, thick hair. Her torso is drenched
with blood, her wrists slashed and her throat slit. There's blood
everywhere, rivulets running down the bathtub, splattering the

tiles, the walls, the sink, the mirror, the towels, dried blood, dark brown, a stale cloying smell. One arm is hanging over the edge of the bath, and beneath the dangling hand, lying in a pool of brown blood on the floor, is a wide open razor. The concierge shrieks. Noria grabs her by the shoulders and steers her into the living room, sits her down in an armchair facing the windows, where she stays sobbing. She hears Bonfils vomiting his guts out in the kitchen. For only his second corpse, this occasion was hardly an anti-climax.

She swings into action. A call to the cops at the High Court. Everyone will be there within fifteen minutes. Bonfils is splashing water on his face in the kitchen. *I've still a few minutes to myself here. Time to check out the apartment.* The first bedroom, the magistrate's, no doubt. Impeccably tidy, and fairly spartan. A narrow bed, two huge wardrobes, a bookcase, not many books, and a magnificent mahogany English writing desk that's out of keeping with the rest of the furniture. Lying on the desk is a fat notebook bound in yellow leather. Noria opens it using the tip of her nail and flicks through the pages. Neat, close handwriting, in felt-tip pen, stilted phrases, jumbled, no points of reference, it looks like a disjointed personal diary. Bonfils joins the concierge in the living room. They can hear the lift operating, the cops arriving. Without thinking, Noria takes the diary and secretes it in the inside pocket of her anorak.

♣

The black BMW saloon with tinted windows leaves the underground car park in avenue Foch and heads towards Mado's building. Sitting in the back, side by side, are Cecchi, in a navy-blue suit and a diagonally striped tie, and Mado, in a grey trouser suit, chatting about this and that. In front are the driver and the bodyguard, paying attention to the road.

'Bornand dropped by last night to try out Katryn's replacement. He agrees with me, she's not up to the job. Too heavily into fucking and not enough class,' is Mado's opinion.

'Well, send her to Amédée, and find another girl. There's no shortage, as far as I know. Did you talk about Katryn's murder?'

'Briefly. He doesn't know that Fernandez shot her.'

'He can't keep his men in line.' He leans over to her with a smile. 'I know you find him charming, elegant ...'

'He's a loyal customer.'

Cecchi looks doubtful:

'Was. Right now, he's pushing his luck. According to Fernandez, only yesterday he refused to use his influence on behalf of the gambling club. As he's having problems with this Chardon dossier ... Didn't I tell you? I got hold of the dossier, through that faggot at *Combat Présent*, very accommodating, the poofter ... I'll find a way of putting pressure on Bornand ... You, in the meantime, keep away from him. I don't want to see him in your lounge any more.'

The BMW pulls up in front of Mado's place.

'Wait here for me. I'll see Madame upstairs and I'll be back down.'

In Mado's office is an answering machine, connected to a line whose number is strictly private and which changes monthly. Cecchi presses the button to play back the message. *A man's voice, muffled by a handkerchief, you can't be too careful, speaks in a flat voice. He must be reading from notes.*

'The investigation into Chardon continues to progress. He still hasn't been located, and the Intelligence Service states that it has had no contact from him these past few days. But he has been identified as the purchaser, two years ago, of the pearl worn by Fatima Rashed at the time of her murder, which confirms that they had a regular relationship going back some time.' Cecchi groans. *Regular relationship going back some time, and I wasn't aware of it. High time to review my organisation.* 'What's more, the Crime Squad found Fatima Rashed's diary and keys at his place. Which makes it all the more vital to find Chardon, prime witness and perhaps more. The Crime Squad is systematically going through all the papers confiscated from his house. They've already identified one of his friends, a certain Beauchamp, and currently the head of security for an arms manufacturer, the SEA.' Cecchi's heart starts racing. *The SEA, the Chardon affair.* The man clears his throat and continues. 'Beauchamp is not unknown to the Drugs Squad. His name has come up several times in connection with the smuggling of Lebanese heroin into Europe via Gabon and Côte-d'Ivoire, the same as that found at Chardon's house, without anything specific ever being pinned on him. He was questioned during the investigation, but he had a cast-iron alibi: the day the prostitute was killed, he worked at the SEA until late into the evening, alibi confirmed by a number of employees. Cleared for the time being. That's the latest.'

And the phone goes dead.

Beauchamp, heroin, the SEA, so that's Chardon's source. Bornand hasn't identified it. The Crime Squad hasn't made the connection between Katryn's murder and the Iranian arms deals. I'm several steps ahead of the lot of them, and with the war between the police departments, I'll be ahead of the game for a while. And I'm determined to make the most of it.

Cecchi immediately erases the message and turns to Mado: 'Here's the ideal opportunity. This time, I shan't pass anything on to Bornand. I've got a treasure trove, and I'm keeping it, and I'm going to use it all for myself, like a big boy. Make me a coffee, then I'll be off. I've got things to do. I shan't be coming to pick you up tonight. Call a taxi.'

❧

Noria goes home. At last. The end of an exhausting day. She'd had to console the concierge, comfort Bonfils, answer the Crime Squad's questions precisely, without it being easy to explain why and how they were there, with Bonfils almost incoherent, go over all their movements, see the body in the bathroom again. And wait for the results of the autopsy.

According to the pathologist, the elderly woman appeared to have died from an embolism, some time on Wednesday, 4 December, between midday and five p.m. – in any case before the magistrate arrived home from the law courts. The magistrate could have committed suicide: the pathologist insists that it is possible to commit suicide by slitting one's own throat. Given the shape of the wound and the position of the razor, in this case, it was even highly likely. The Crime Squad reckon that the magistrate learned she'd been taken off the case, went home depressed (the clerk confirms that is the case) and discovered her mother dead. So the suicide theory is highly plausible. The door and windows are locked from the inside, there are no signs of an intrusion, three people including two cops were there when the door was opened, suicide is certain, and the inquest will soon be over.

She does not switch on the light, but walks over to the window. The city is shrouded in mist and darkness. The Eiffel Tower is barely visible despite its illuminations, and La Défense not at all. The neon lights of the Grand Rex cinema are off, it must be after eleven p.m. She can hear the muffled noise of the traffic, quietly reassuring.

No hurry, she needs time to recover. First of all, a bath, feet resting on the rim of the tub, hair piled loosely on top of her head. No massage glove today, everything soft and gentle, take things easy. She lingers in the warmth of the bathroom, brushes her hair for ages, a ritual she finds relaxing, splashes on some eau de cologne and slips into a towelling bathrobe that's several sizes too big for her. Then she puts away some clothes that are piled on a chair, makes the bed and gives the shelves a quick dust to remove the biscuit crumbs. She goes into her tiny kitchen, which is less than basic. Here there are never dishes simmering for hours, hissing, the smell of which reawakens family nightmares. She makes herself a steaming chocolate and butters a few slices of bread, which she places on her little Formica table. Next to the magistrate's notebook. She can't delay the moment of confrontation any longer.

Noria shudders. She touches the yellow leather cover and inhales its odour, to convince herself that it really is there. Because it shouldn't be on her kitchen table. Curiosity, wanting to know. What? The fascination of that naked body, lying in the bathtub with its throat slit. Sensing violence, the violence of a woman, so close, the same as me, all warm, in the pit of her stomach. And vertigo. She visualises the movement, the razor, and suddenly, blood gushing everywhere, spurting onto the walls, the tiled floor, that self-destructive rage, she feels herself to be in danger.

And Bonfils. Flashback: in the lobby, on familiar terrain. A good-looking guy, his lips parted, lightly defined. Charming and hazy. Flashback: in the kitchen, on the brink of the abyss. Where's he in all this?

The yellow notebook: she must pluck up the courage to open it.

She skims the pages quickly.

... Every time I come in or go out, I hear her double-turn each of the three locks, one after the other, the metal shutters clang down over the windows, noises I find heart-rending, day after day ... and the minute I'm out, all I can think of is getting back as quickly as possible, behind the bars ...

... Jeanne is preserving her energy, she never leaves the apartment any more ('I don't want to die away from home'), eats very little, scarcely breathes, all her energy goes into her determination to live, with a sort of fury, like a daily rebuke ... She's there, all the time, she invades me, she suffocates me, she says: you're abandoning me ... Impossible to focus my mind ...

... Legs heavy, heart pounding, tiny veins on her thighs have burst creating red and blue filaments. An imaginary landscape ...

... Mother and daughter facing each other. Absolute solitude, shared loathing. Jeanne is only interested in the weather. Clouds, sun, rain, the darkness – which fell very early today, the only dimension of history that is still accessible to her. I can't bring myself to talk to her any more ... Thoughts pass, like fleeting images, instantly forgotten ... Her or me? ...

... I look at my hands, the joints inescapably becoming deformed, like hers ... I'm losing my grip, I feel as if nothing imprints itself on my memory any more, time is monotonous, ravaged. What cases did I read yesterday? Who did I meet? I have to piece together my memories from scattered clues. And frequently, I fail ... Over the Rashed case, this afternoon, moments of confusion, as if my muddled thoughts were only

holding together thanks to a huge effort of concentration. If I give way a little, everything disintegrates …

Noria gets her breath back. She hears the distorted echo of her own nightmares. *But I got out, I saved my life.* She stretches, massages her face and goes over to the window. *The city, as always.* And sits down to finish reading.

The last entry is very different:

At work, Simone put a phone call through to me: the Dupuis and Martenot law firm. Why did I take the call? I knew exactly what was going to happen. Lack of resolve, of self-confidence, as before. Nicolas greets me very politely, asks after my health, then my mother's. Ten years since we last saw each other. Then he informs me that Mado is one of his clients. I already know this. That she won't respond to my summons. As I've seen. And kindly warns me that incriminating Mado will upset a lot of people in high places. I hate him with every fibre of my being.

Noria closes the diary. The magistrate hated right to the death. Bonfils, not a word about him in all these pages. He's somewhere else, a blip. And a mystery man, this Nicolas who played a part in the magistrate's suicide. He's protecting Mado who Katryn worked for, and Katryn was trying to blackmail one of Mado's clients. This guy is somehow linked to the murder. *What do I do with this information?*

Three o'clock in the morning, much too early to wait for sunrise. *To bed now, and we'll see what tomorrow brings.*

Saturday 7 December

In a little studio flat belonging to Mado in a quiet apartment building in the well-heeled 16th *arrondissement*, Karim sits naked in a low, deep, winged armchair smugly contemplating his bulging paunch, the line of curly black hairs running down from his navel and his flaccid penis resting on the red and white striped velvet. An afternoon and a night spent fucking two of Mado's girls, perfect as always. And he'd been masterful, he gloats, scratching his testicles. One of the girls brings him a tray which she sets down on the coffee table beside him. She's wearing a short navy-blue silk pyjama shirt, with nothing underneath it. He slips his hand between her thighs and fondles her crotch, then attacks his breakfast. English-style. His favourite: astringent tea, bitter-tasting, toast and marmalade, freshly-squeezed grapefruit juice. A sigh of contentment. The girls have vanished into the bathroom.

Another reason for his complacency is yesterday's meeting with Bornand, not half as tough as he'd expected. The lost plane was an excuse to edge him out. He proved to be a real pushover. That was unexpected.

Better watch the time: he mustn't miss the flight to Beirut.

He gets up and ambles lazily into the bedroom, dragging his feet, calls the other girl, the one wearing a basque revealing her generous breasts, and has her dress him while he buries his face and hands in her bosom. Then he sends her away with a slap on the buttocks.

'Call me a taxi.'

Alone in the bedroom, he checks the contents of his leather briefcase: the papers he'd been planning to use to put pressure on Bornand. He hadn't needed them. A few hours' work in Beirut, and the whole affair will be closed. He checks his appearance in the mirror: impeccable.

'A white Mercedes will pick you up within a few minutes,' says the girl.

He says his goodbyes, his hands roaming everywhere, and leaves, feeling elated.

Outside the building, a white Mercedes is waiting, its engine idling. The driver steps out and opens the door for him.

'Roissy.'

'Very good, sir.'

He gets in, the door slams, and the taxi pulls away quickly. Karim vaguely notices that there's a glass partition between him and the driver, which is unusual for a Parisian taxi. He opens his leather briefcase, leafs through some papers, reliving the night he has just spent. Mado's establishment really is top class.

The taxi doesn't seem to be taking the most direct route. Usually ... He leans over to the glass partition. It's fixed shut. He raps twice. The driver doesn't respond. He looks at it more closely. Toughened glass. Sits down again. The rear windows are tinted and appear to be of toughened glass too. He presses the control switch. Nothing moves. Grabs a door handle. Locked. A moment of panic. Bangs the windows and rattles the handles, in vain. Sits back. *What's going on? The taxi: the girl called it. The girls: work for Mado. Mado: a great friend of Bornand's. And her pimp, caught sight of him a couple of times, a notorious gangster ... Is it possible?*

The Mercedes drives fast, there's little traffic on a Saturday morning, they're already on the motorway heading south. The driver turns off onto an empty secondary road heading deep into the forest.

Scared out of his wits, Karim pisses himself.

♣

At the wheel of his metallic grey Porsche, Nicolas Martenot heads for home. He drives slowly in the direction of Paris. An eighteen-hole round of golf at the Saint-Cloud club, a session in the sauna, a quick lunch, then a long game of bridge with plenty of booze which he'd won hands down. And yet, alone in his luxury car, he has a sense of unease triggered by the call from the police yesterday informing him of his ex-wife's suicide. He says her name out aloud: *Laura Luccioni. She slit her throat. Remorse? ... It was her choice. As it had been her choice to be a magistrate. And to believe in it. Good, evil. Frigid. Her icy distance scared me, fascinated me even. The ultimate inaccessible woman, and morally upright into the bargain.* He can still hear Bornand's voice, in the spacious lounge in his apartment at the foot of the Eiffel Tower: 'Your wife is an uptight pain in the arse. She'll make your life a misery.' He'll have to cancel all his appointments on Monday and go to the funeral. Half the law courts will be there. Her throat slit. Martenot shudders. And sees Françoise's face, contorted by something akin to hatred. *Hatred. Why hatred? For me?* Women's violence, impossible to cope with. The feeling of unease grows more acute. Bornand's doing. A snatch of a refrain keeps going round and round, like the chorus of a ditty: power, politics, sexual dysfunction.

I don't think it's my thing.

Irritated, he turns on the radio. Newsflash: 'Two fire bombs have exploded in Paris department stores. One went off in the china department of the Galeries Lafayette, at five thirty p.m., and the other, in the leather goods department of Au Printemps, twenty minutes later. Initial reports state that around fifty people have been injured, ten of them seriously. No one appears to have been killed. The bombs were home-made incendiary devices. The police think it was probably the act of a loner or someone mentally unstable, or an act of vengeance.' *Come off it! Disinformation or incompetence? In the heat of the moment it's guesswork, of course, but after all, it's barely a week since the plane disappeared. Iran's at war with France again.* 'Given that the bombs exploded at peak shopping time on a Saturday afternoon, two weeks before Christmas, it is a miracle that the toll, albeit provisional, is no higher. The police estimate that there were nearly a hundred thousand people in and around the stores, making it difficult for the emergency services to get through. By eight p.m., all the wounded had been evacuated, but the area is still completely sealed off, and the police are currently urging motorists driving through the centre of Paris to avoid the right bank.'

Feeling powerless and bitter, Martenot switches off the radio and bangs the steering wheel with the palm of his hand in rage. *What a mess. That's it. I'm dropping Bornand. He's finished. My firm's interests first. It'll be a relief.*

He smiles: the ritual murder of the father. About time too, at my age.

Monday 9 December

The New York-Paris night flight. Bornand lands at Roissy without having slept, feeling pretty groggy. He buys the newspapers and repairs to the airport bar, amid the hubbub of comings and goings. A strong double espresso and two pills, just to wake him up.

Paris Turf, first of all, to read the commentary on Crystal Palace's triumph yesterday at Longchamp, in the group 3 race. A clear win, by two lengths. The makings of a champion. He closes his eyes, the Aigles track at dawn, smells the horses' powerful odour after exertion, hears them snorting. A mirage …

And the national press. The headlines are devoted to Saturday's bomb attacks. It didn't take the Iranians long to react. Idiotic editorials claiming it to be the work of a deranged loner! The mind boggles. He turns to the financial section. In one column, he finds the article he's expecting:

Rumours of bankruptcy in Beirut.

The International Bank of Lebanon is the biggest private bank in the Middle East. With a presence in the region's many arms markets, it is also the biggest investment bank for oil magnates to deposit their private fortunes, and therefore has close ties with the leading banks in the London, New York and Geneva financial markets.

Until now, it had managed to avoid the devastating effects of the Lebanon war, by striking a balance within its board of directors between the different Lebanese communities and between the Syrians and the Gulf states. That was its real success story.

It seems that this era is over. In the past few days, several of the bank's major customers, whose investments are highly volatile, have begun to close their accounts. If this trend continues, it is likely to force the bank to sell off some of its property assets, in a highly unfavourable market.

To make matters worse, one of the bank's main partners, the Franco-Lebanese Walid Karim, vanished three days ago, taking with him certain confidential documents relating to the current crisis ... The fate of the IBL should become clear by the end of the week.

Bornand folds the papers, stretches his legs, pulls back his shoulders and his arms. Karim. *A chapter of my life unravelling. Sinister. His choice, not mine. Business will resume with Iran, this time with the Americans. They need the IBL as much as I need them. The hostages ... It's not for want of trying.* And floating guiltily around in his mind is the thought that the longer the embargo lasts, the better it is for business. He contemplates the crowds milling around him.

When he arrives in his office, Bornand finds a number of messages, one of which says: 'Call Flandin back urgently.' He wrinkles his nose. *The boss of the SEA, a hysterical panic-monger. What can he want to talk to me about that's so urgent? A bad omen.*

On the phone, Flandin sounds at the end of his tether, his voice cracking uncontrollably.

'Have you read the *Tribune de Lille*?'

'No. I'm not interested in that kind of local paper.'

'Then you're wrong. I shall therefore have the pleasure of reading you an article from the front page of today's *Tribune*. Are you listening?'

Bornand pours himself a whisky, sits down and sighs:

'I'm listening.'

'It's entitled: *Mystery plane crash*.'

'In true provincial press style,' thinks Bornand.

Flandin continues: 'This is the article:

On 29 November 1985, Turkey signalled the disappearance of a Boeing 747 cargo plane in its airspace, in the vicinity of Lake Van. So far, no airline company has reported the disappearance of one of its planes, nobody seems bothered about the death of the crew of possibly three, four, five or more people about whom we know nothing, not even their nationality. The owner(s) of the cargo have not come forward either to demand an investigation or to request compensation. And as the explosion took place at the start of winter, over a semi-desert in a perilous mountainous region, no doubt it will take a long time before a team of investigators from the Turkish civil aviation authority completes a report on this incident.

It was tempting to try and find out more about this mysterious plane. When the Ankara air-traffic controllers took charge on 29 November, the flight plan showed that it had taken off from Malta at 09.30, destination Tehran, with a cargo of rice.

Admittedly, operations at Valetta are still disrupted, flights have only just resumed after the tragic ending of the hijacking of the Egypt Air Boeing which left dozens dead,[7] but the information supplied by the control tower at Valetta is categorical: no Boeing 747 cargo had taken off at 09.30.

However, at that same time, a Boeing 747 cargo from Brussels-Zavantem had flown over Malta and came under the authority of the Valetta air-traffic controllers, who gave it a new flight number and directed it towards Iran. Brussels-Zavantem Airport confirms that the Boeing 747 cargo took off at 06.58, destination Malta-Valetta. According to the customs declarations, it was carrying electronic equipment belonging to the SAPA. Hence of course the interest in finding out more about this equipment. The SAPA is a very recently formed company whose registered office is in the Bahamas. It purchased the cargo of electronic equipment on 28 November, i.e. the day before the Boeing crashed, from the SEA, a French company based in the Paris region and specialising in electronic equipment and arms. The SAPA itself is merely a dummy company for the SEA, to ensure that the name of the SEA does not appear officially in the transaction, so that it is harder to establish the true nature of this 'electronic equipment'. Earlier this year, the SEA successfully bought up a number of Magic 550 missiles that had been decommissioned by the French army. The reason officially given is to recycle the onboard electronic equipment. Could it be that those same missiles were now en route to Iran? Watch this space.'

A long silence.

'What do you think about that, Bornand?'

'It's very badly written.'

Flandin roars:

'You guaranteed me absolute confidentiality. You've totally fucked up!' his words are coming out in a jumbled rush. 'I want to protect my company, that's the only thing I care about. I'm not going to sacrifice it to bail you out. I'm meeting the journalist from the *Tribune* this afternoon. He's going to be so interested in what I'm going to tell him that he won't bother about the SEA any more. All the bribes paid to the ministerial staff and to the Defence Ministry, the five million francs for them to turn a blind eye to the sale of the Magic 550s. I've got names. I don't know what they did with the money afterwards … I'm going to tell that journalist that the SAPA is you, and only you, something he doesn't seem to be aware of, and that this operation was to net you thirty million francs …'

Bornand fidgets. He can't allow this maniac to cramp his style. *I was right.*

'Calm down, Flandin. I assure you the SEA has very little to fear. At worst, a bit of fuss in the press, but the Ministry won't prosecute, as you well know. You're meeting your journalist this afternoon, OK. Only let's have lunch together beforehand to talk things over. And let's try and avoid the worst. We've all got something to lose in this affair. One o'clock at Laurent's, in one of the private dining rooms on the first floor?'

A long silence.

'I'll be there.'

The crisis defused, Bornand hangs up. *That's the danger of working with beginners, they lack nerve. Contact Beauchamp, that's why I brought him in.* He calls the SEA security department. Beauchamp hasn't come in this morning, nor has he called in to leave a message. Bornand phones him at home and gets the answering machine. He hasn't put in an appearance at his regular bar, a favourite haunt of African mercenaries, for the past three days. Worrying.

Bornand stands up and gazes out over the rooftops. Silence, which infuses him slowly and turns into a sense of solitude tinged with anxiety. *Must find out what's going on with the Djimils. Four days ago, I had everything sorted, the affair was buried. Who's stirring things up again? The Intelligence Service, of course. It's the only possible explanation. They've declared outright war on me. I'll make them sorry. But first of all, I've got to deal with Flandin, even if it takes a bit of improvisation.* He looks at his watch. Nine a.m. And Martenot's wife's funeral is at twelve. Not a second to lose.

When Fernandez comes into the office he finds Bornand, reclining in his armchair, his face pale and his eyes closed, looking as if he's asleep. Fernandez falters. Bornand sits up, looks at him and smiles:

'It's nothing, tiredness, jet lag. You're having lunch with me today, young fellow. We're going to meet Flandin. I've booked a private dining room at Laurent's.'

Fernandez is staggered. In four years, this is the first time that Bornand has taken him to what appears to be a business lunch, and this blurring of roles is baffling.

♣

The two hearses arrive in convoy at the main entrance to Père-Lachaise cemetery. They take the left-hand avenue flanked by tombstones leading up to the funeral parlour. A procession forms and follows behind. Noria Ghozali walks beside Bonfils. All around, there's little emotion, the gathering appears to be made up of officials, magistrates, lawyers, police officers, and a few strangers. Impressive 'institutional' wreaths. Handshakes between cops and magistrates. Walking alone at the head of the procession is a man in his forties, athletic, dark, hair on the long side, good-looking. Towards the back, Noria spots Simone, the clerk, head bowed and tears in her eyes. She slips in beside her, takes her arm. There's a moment of uncertainty, then the clerk recognises her and leans on her for support.

'Alone, completely alone,' she murmurs.

The magistrate? Her? Both of them?

'Who's the man at the front?' asks Noria quietly.

The clerk looks up for a second, and bows her head again.

'Nicolas Martenot. They were married. They divorced about ten years ago. Now, he's one of the top corporate lawyers in Paris. A shark and a regular on the night-club circuit. She ended up hating him.'

'Did they see much of each other?'

'No, never.' They walk in silence. The clerk continues, a slight hesitation in her voice: 'An out-and-out bastard.'

'He was involved in having her taken off the case …' Noria's words hang in the air, intimating a question.

'I'm sure he was.' Then, with a start: 'What makes you say that?'

Noria dodges the question.

'And the magistrate thought that Mado had something to do with Fatima Rashed's murder?'

'Listen, to be honest, I have absolutely no idea about that. My feeling is that she was going after Mado because of the challenge. Why do you ask me that?'

The procession has reached the open grave. A deep vault, two coffins already at the bottom of the cavity. This is the end of a family history. Simone wipes her eyes. Noria takes advantage of the moment to step back and join Bonfils. An impasse. Not surprisingly.

Martenot throws in the first handfuls of earth, and the flowers, then receives people's condolences, without putting on a big act of mourning. Nor does anyone else as a matter of fact.

Noria closes her eyes and has a flashback of the blood-soaked body in the bathtub. When she opens them again, the clerk has disappeared.

People gather in small knots at the exit, waiting for their chauffeur-driven cars, exchanging a few words, taking out their engagement diaries. Noria and Bonfils stand to one side. Noria watches Martenot as he goes from group to group, smiling, urbane. He greets a couple, the man in his sixties, tall, very slim, with a long, mobile face and a white moustache, she younger, barely forty, a decorative blonde, sophisticated chignon and make-up, in a rather theatrical black overcoat. On seeing Martenot coming towards them, she starts as if to turn away, possibly to avoid him; the man suddenly freezes, grabs her arm and pins her brutally to his side. The woman sways. Noria feels his fingers digging into her flesh through the fabric. The couple exchange a few sentences with Martenot who moves on to another group. A few metres away, a man is in conversation with the clerk who points at Noria and Bonfils. He makes his way towards them.

'Inspector Dumont, Police Intelligence, Paris Section. Superintendent Macquart is expecting you in his office at headquarters at two p.m. this afternoon. He'll inform your superiors.'

Bonfils' jaw drops in surprise. Noria drags him away.

'Let's go and have lunch, we've just got time. I need to talk to you.'

♣

A luxury private dining room lavishly decorated in shades of sea-green with two vast windows overlooking the gardens of the

Champs-Élysées and a circular table laid for three. Bornand, extremely elegant in a pale grey, immaculately fitting worsted suit and a dark grey silk and wool tie, is pacing up and down, waiting for his guest, his face expressionless. Fernandez, stands stiffly in a corner, on the alert, trying to keep a low profile.

Flandin arrives accompanied by Beauchamp. Bornand shivers. *Impossible to get hold of, Beauchamp? He tricked me. Chardon ... Lebanese heroin ... Beauchamp too. The dossier, it's him. Both of them working for Intelligence? It's possible. The Djimils, a red herring? So what about Moricet? Danger. Too late to back out, take things as they come.*

Bornand warmly shakes his guests' hands and introduces Fernandez, joking: 'My head of staff, if I had a staff', has another place laid, and asks the maître d'hôtel to serve the aperitif. A glance around the room. Two bodyguards for guests – this was how politics and business was conducted in Paris, in the winter of 1985 ...

'What will you have to drink, my friend?'

'Whisky. A light Scotch, neat.'

'Same for me.'

Once the drinks have been poured, Bornand goes over to the window and gazes out over the Champs Elysées in the greyness and the cold, then returns to his guests. He signals to Fernandez that he should take care of Beauchamp then joins Flandin, steering him over to one of the windows.

'Sad, Paris at this time of year.' Flandin, his face drawn, lets him speak, without reacting. 'I'm just back from the USA, with some interesting opportunities.' Still no response. Bornand puts his glass down next to a huge bouquet of flowers on a pedestal table between the two windows, and takes a long envelope from his inside pocket. *Specific proposals, in writing and* with figures. He proffers the envelope to Flandin. 'I'm simply asking you to read these documents after lunch, before going to see your journalist.'

Flandin, a little taken aback, wavers for a moment, then puts his glass down on the table and takes the envelope, turns it over and over, then folds it and puts it in his pocket. Bornand has already picked up Flandin's glass, while Flandin picks up the one left on the pedestal table. Then they both make their way over to the centre of the room where Fernandez is engaging Beauchamp in conversation as best he can:

'We've met before …'

Beauchamp snaps:

'I'd be very surprised. We don't move in the same circles.'

Fernandez, very ill at ease, feels a crazy urge to beat the shit out of Bornand who raises his glass with a smile.

'Come, whatever happens, let's drink to the success of our venture, it's not too late.'

Shortly after, Flandin follows suit, takes one, then another slug of whisky, and suddenly stiffens, his mouth open. Noise-lessly, his face drawn and mottled, he slowly slumps to the floor and lies in a contorted heap. Bornand watches him collapse from high above, from a long way away, almost surprised. Flashback: another body, long ago, killed in a courtyard, and he himself kicking the body relentlessly. *No comparison, this death is sanitised.* He leans over to retrieve the envelope he's just given Flandin. Then it's all stations go. Fernandez rushes over to perform cardiac massage. Beauchamp calls the waiters. The ambulance, the cops, the room fills with people. The words 'heart attack' are on everyone's lips.

Bornand, stock still, contemplates the scene. *I'm spared the gourmet lunch.*

§

Bonfils and Noria Ghozali enter Macquart's office. It is very ordinary looking, unlike the man sitting at his desk ready to ambush them. Leaning slightly forward, his forearms resting on the desk, his broad, stubby hands folded, he scrutinises them, without making a movement. He has a round, fleshy face, very thin lips, and a fixed, expressionless stare. He's a little on the corpulent side without being fat, and wears his hair plastered back along with a salt-and-pepper moustache trimmed very short. He's wearing a navy blue three-piece suit with very thin white stripes, a white shirt and a tie. The archetypal civil servant, with a slightly 1950s touch. Noria instinctively thinks: *a real killer.* Instinctively she says to herself: *a cop who commands respect.* Instinctively thinks: *my lucky day.*

He motions them to sit down, allowing a silence to hover as he gazes at them, then eventually says:

'Why is it that two junior cops from the 19th *arrondissement* are so interested in Maître Martenot?'

Straight to the point, and fast. The clerk must be working for Intelligence. Impressive. Noria and Bonfils have prepared their answer, Noria insists on taking the lead.

'I was the only one to take an interest in Maître Martenot.'

Macquart looks from Noria to Bonfils and back at Noria who takes the yellow notebook from the inside pocket of her anorak, opens it at the last page. She leans over and places it on Macquart's desk.

'The magistrate's personal diary.'

He reads the open page, flicks through the rest, stony-faced, closes it and puts it away in a drawer.

'Where did you find that?'

'In the magistrate's apartment, on the day we found her body.'

'And you kept it to yourself. Need I say more?' *Two smart, ambitious young cops, completely out of control. They could cause havoc in sensitive cases. Do I break them or bring them on board?* 'And while you're at it, tell me how you came to be in the magistrate's apartment too.'

'We were involved in the identification of Fatima Rashed …'

'I am aware of your connection with that case.'

'… At that point, we thought there could have been a second man in the restaurant with Chardon and Fatima Rashed. That same man could have picked Chardon up in Fatima Rashed's car, just after her murder, and that was the last time Chardon was seen, alive or dead.'

This girl, with her impenetrable dark eyes and taut body, possessed of a raw strength.

'Go on.'

'We wrote a report and we took it to the magistrate at the law courts.'

'She wasn't there.'

'The clerk gave us her address.'

'I don't think so.'

Bonfils breaks his silence and says with a dazzling smile:

'I found the magistrate a fascinating woman. One evening, I followed her home.' He takes the additional report out of his pocket and places it in front of Macquart. 'After her death, the investigation was put on hold and nobody's asked us for anything further.'

'So I'm the first person to see this report?'

'That's correct.'

He takes his time reading it. *Good work. Excellent work. My mind's made up. I bring them on board.*

'Would you be interested in a transfer to Intelligence?'

'Yes,' says Noria.

'No,' says Bonfils.

Macquart smiles, for the first time.

'Just as I thought.' Then, turning to Noria: 'Why is the superintendent of the 19th so happy to see the back of you?'

Noria, her hands clasped on her knee, tense, her knuckles white, reflects for a second.

'I think he's afraid of me.'

Macquart rises, shows them to the door of his office and says, with a hand on Bonfils' shoulder:

'For your own good, if you don't want to pay for her mistakes, forget the whole thing, Bonfils, including your latest report.'

'I already have.'

'And you, Ghozali, eight o'clock tomorrow morning in my office.'

As soon as Noria and Bonfils have left his office, Macquart calls in one of his inspectors.

'Laurencin, drop what you're working on. I have an emergency. I'm giving you this packet of photos, which you are going to show a few people. If the result confirms my suspicions, you can cancel all leave.'

Noria and Bonfils leave the office together and set off down the street with a sigh of relief. They walk quickly away, side by side, their heads down. Noria's expression is inscrutable. But when he brushes against her, Bonfils feels the explosive tension in her muscles. They go into the Soleil d'Or, which is almost empty at this hour, and sit at the back of the café. A hot chocolate for Noria, a beer for Bonfils. He looks up at her.

'Do you know what you're letting yourself in for? The political police, champions of dirty tricks.'

She replies aggressively:

'I'm not like you. I don't have any choice, and I'm in a hurry.'

Then a smile. In a single movement, she undoes her chignon and loosens her hair. The shining, black, undulating mass spreads over her shoulders, sculpts her round cheeks, offsets her features. She stands up, presses her hands down on the table and leans towards him. She places her mouth on his upper lip and licks it with the moist tip of her tongue, the trace of white foam leaving a slight tickling sensation, her breath coming in warm, short bursts. A brief silence, then Bonfils, incredulous, says:

'Now what happens?'

'Forget the whole thing, Bonfils, forget the whole thing.'

And she ditches him there, at the table, with the beer and the chocolate, rushing out as fast as her legs will carry her.

♣

'Bestégui? … Good to hear you, I was just about to call you. Where are you? At home?'

' … '

'Yes, that's correct, Flandin has just died of a heart attack … While we were having lunch together …'

' … '

'Rumour! What nonsense. The burial certificate has already been issued. It was the article in the *Tribune de Lille* that killed him. Have you read it?'

' … '

'I know it's the dossier you had in your hands.' Bornand's voice is strained, aggressive, veering towards the shrill rather more than he would wish. 'That's what I wanted to talk to you about. Do you know a certain Chardon?'

'...'

'And do you know who you are employing? A pimp, black-mailer and drug trafficker. Not exactly a brilliant move.'

'...'

'Of course I have proof. A prostitute was murdered ten days ago and Chardon is mixed up in it somehow. The Crime Squad is investigating him and they've uncovered the full extent of his activities. You can easily check, I'm sure you've got your con-tacts at Crime Squad HQ. They also have proof that Chardon works for your paper. It's not certain they'll use it, but you never know ...'

'...'

'The best bit is still to come, André. Chardon is in the pay of the Intelligence Service.'

'...'

Bornand sniggers:

'His nose in your shit. The real question is: who dug up the Chardon dossier, which was well and truly buried three days ago? And the answer can only be: the Intelligence Service.'

'...'

'No, I'm not out of my mind. Chardon is involved in a heroin trafficking ring with a certain Beauchamp, head of security at the SEA. You know what I'm talking about, because you've had the dossier in your hands. He's the source of the information. When the prostitute was murdered – I have no idea why, by the way – Chardon got scared. Intelligence covered up for him, either by hiding or by murdering him ...'

'...'

Bornand, exasperated, bangs his fist down on the desk:

'Oh yes, of course it's possible. Don't act more naive than you are. Two months ago, your paper ran a press campaign on the Irish of Vincennes ... I'm not blaming you, but remember, your informer, your only informer, was dealt with by military security. And now Intelligence have Chardon. These people hate us, André. The official police departments are poisoned by our political enemies. And besides, their sights are set directly on me, because through me, they're targeting the Élysée unit, the *bête noire* of all the official police departments, because it's the living proof of their ineffectiveness ... What we are witnessing, André, is a police coup, and I'm weighing my words carefully, here. I don't intend to let them get away with it. I need you, you can't abandon me.'

When Bestégui hangs up, he is deeply disturbed. Paranoid, Bornand? Not totally, it would seem. So many facts stack up ... His tone is violent, the threats barely disguised. But how to get away from him? Sooner or later, it'll be payback time and the other version will surface. Ultimately, we're in the same boat.

This must all be wrapped up by tomorrow evening. There's just enough time to get down to work.

♣

Laurencin walks into the Brasserie des Sports at around five p.m. The customers are crowding around the bar, but only a few tables are occupied in the hushed atmosphere of the main restaurant. A few elderly ladies sit drinking tea. He introduces himself to the owner, who greets him warmly, offers him a pastis and asks how the investigation is going.

'It's going, it's going …' he replies vaguely. 'I've got a few photos I'd like to show one of your waiters, I won't keep him long …'

He sits at a round table on the terrace, glass in hand. Roger comes over to join him. Laurencin places a set of around thirty black and white photos of men's faces in front him.

'Take your time.'

Roger leans forward, concentrating hard ('I'm not sure I'd recognise him, you know'), examines all the photos, goes back to one he's already looked at several times, and ends up choosing two possibilities. One is the photo of Fernandez, the Intelligence cop seconded to Bornand's personal service. Macquart will be happy. There goes his leave.

❧

Around the middle of the afternoon, Fernandez steps out of Laurent's into the Champs-Élysée gardens, the cold air whipping his face. It is already beginning to grow dark and the lights are coming on. He starts walking straight ahead in the direction of the Étoile, into the bright flickering lights, into the crowds. He still hasn't digested the shock. Knocked for six, his mind in a state of total confusion, with three little words going round and round obsessively: *a fuck-up, a fuck-up*. He walks faster, enjoying being jostled by the stream of pedestrians come to see the illuminations or to do their Christmas shopping. He slowly gathers his wits. By the time he reaches the Étoile, he starts thinking more coherently. *Bornand didn't trust Flandin. He contacted Beauchamp, and between them they killed Flandin.* His astonishment when it happened: a piece of acting. *How they did it, I have no idea, but they killed him, and Bornand used me as a witness, to make the heart attack credible. It's the only reason he invited me to lunch.* A deep breath. *That much at least is for certain.* And if Bornand has sunk to that level, he's finished.

He strides along and starts making his way around the vast place de l'Étoile, crossing avenues Wagram and Mac-Mahon at the traffic lights. *If Bornand's finished, that means I am too. All the dirty tricks will come to light when the boss has gone. Four years, an age. And always under pressure. Not sure I can remember everything.*

He walks up avenue Foch in the direction of porte Dauphine, with no specific destination in mind. *Go back to Intelligence …. Out of the question … They hate Bornand. Or Cecchi … Maybe go and pick up a high-class whore on the avenue … Mado's, can't even consider it for quite a while …* and he stops in front of the building where Cecchi lives. He sits on a bench. Another certainty*: It's Cecchi who got the* Tribune de Lille *to publish the article in order to put pressure on Bornand, who doesn't realise it yet. Cecchi's going to use me as go-between, he's got me, and it's hell. Caught between the two of them, I'll never survive … I'm up shit creek … but if Bornand's finished, that only leaves Cecchi …* Fernandez sits bolt upright, realising that he's freezing. He knocks back some amphetamines and stands up. He sets off at a slow jog to warm himself up.

♣

Laurencin brings back the photos and some good news: there's a strong chance that Fernandez was at the Brasserie des Sports on the day Katryn was murdered. Macquart savours the news slowly, in silence, his eyes half closed. The man who killed Katryn and probably Chardon too. One final push and the net will close in around Bornand. He sits up.

'Well, Laurencin. Since this morning, there's been an article in the *Tribune de Lille*, and a meal at Laurent's. I'm convinced that Bornand's involved in arms trafficking in one way or another. On that score, we've got nothing on him, and other departments specialising in that area are well ahead of us, especially the National Security Service. But we can take back the initiative in other areas. Bornand is probably implicated, directly or indirectly in two murders. We're going to play Fernandez as our master trump. I'm going to call him into this office as soon as possible. That doesn't preclude us from pursuing other leads. If there's been friction between Bornand and Chardon, knowing Chardon, it must be because there's some vice or drugs business involved. Just to be sure, I called one of my friends in the Drugs Squad, Superintendent Daquin. He confirmed that Bornand's a user, but Cecchi's his regular dealer and there are no problems. No joy there. There's still Bornand's mistress. We have nothing on her in our files, which is a regrettable shortcoming, and I'm counting on you to remedy it. We only know one thing about Françoise Michel: she's deeply attached to her mother who lives in Annecy. She phones her every week and goes to see her several times a year. You'll go there tomorrow morning. Savoie's a lovely region. Dig around and bring back what you can. Preferably on the girl, but also on the mother, it might come in useful.'

Tuesday 10 December

Laurencin's primary target: Antoinette Michel. He has her address and her social security number, and that's about all. He's going to have to improvise. He drives at about ninety-five miles an hour on the motorway; the Morvan flies past in the dark, he needs to get on her case as quickly as possible.

Antoinette Michel lives in a magnificent dark wood chalet built on a white stone base on the slopes of Lake Annecy encircled by mountains. It has a terrace and a balcony looking out over a meadow, a steep slope planted with a few bare fruit trees; far below lies the stone-grey lake. Laurencin, standing still, slowly breathes in the silence and the cold. He turns around. There's a light on in an upstairs room but no sign of movement. At the back of the house is a big garage opening onto the road. He tries the handle. The door is unlocked. He steps inside and glances around. It's tidy and in the centre is a huge Range Rover, its tyres still caked with mud.

A wealthy woman, or at least very comfortably off, a seemingly peaceful existence. For the moment, it's difficult to tell much more, and dangerous to hang around. Time to head for the social security office in Annecy.

♣

The same room as before, already familiar and the same

Macquart, frosty as ever, lying in wait behind his desk. He launches straight into the attack:

'First of all, a few principles. We always work in very small teams. When you're on a case, you only discuss it with your partner and myself and with nobody outside this office, in the force or elsewhere. That's the first ground rule. Rule number two is that everything comes back to me. I want full daily reports. You may have to act in a way that is just within the law, but I'm the one who makes the decisions. And I won't tolerate any exceptions. Understood, Ghozali?' She nods, takes it in her stride without batting an eyelid. 'Intelligence is a rather special branch of the police. Our purpose is to get to the truth.' He thumps his desk lightly to drive home each word. 'The truth wherever it may be, whatever it may be. Is that understood?' Noria nods. 'Then we think how we're going to use it, and again, I'm the one who decides. This isn't the Crime Squad. Crime Squad, never heard of it. Is that clear?'

'It's clear.'

'Good.' He rises. 'I'm going to introduce you to the inspector you'll be working with on this case.'

A small meeting room, fixed up at the end of a corridor, light entering through a Velux skylight. A table and five padded chairs fill the entire space, which is closed off by a soundproofed door. In one corner is a fridge, containing a variety of drinks.

'If you want coffee,' says Macquart, 'you have to go to the machine in the corridor.'

On the table are writing pads, felt-tips, and a jam jar full of squares of chocolate. No ashtrays. A man gets to his feet as they enter. Macquart performs the introductions:

'Inspector Levert. One of the best cops in Intelligence ...'

Mid-thirties, athletic-looking, long, narrow face, with a

prominent nose and a very straight forelock, chestnut hair starting to grey. Instinctively, Noria's antennae pick up macho cop. Watch out.

'… Noria Ghozali, police officer. A new recruit. Tremendous natural ability, in my view, but a lot to learn. I'm counting on you, Milou.'

They sit down. Macquart, relaxed, helps himself to a piece of chocolate and begins.

'First of all, let's review the Fatima Rashed murder, and you'll see that it's a bit different from the Crime Squad's case. Let's begin with Chardon, a journalist involved in all kinds of trafficking and a blackmailer who runs his business with a great deal of wiliness and caution. We've got him, we've had him sentenced for living off immoral earnings, and we can have him locked up any time we choose. For us, he's a mine of information. As soon as the investigation opened, I informed the Crime Squad that he was on our books. A couple of weeks ago, he tells us that people are gossiping about Bornand's mistress. Do you know Bornand? No? He's an advisor to and close friend of the President's, who plays an important and shadowy part in Élysée politics. He's one of the heads of the Élysée unit, the President's private police. In other words, a big fish. The minute his name comes up, the matter needs to be handled with kid gloves. That's why I couldn't allow you to carry on sniffing around undisturbed. But the fact is that Chardon didn't tell us any more about Bornand's mistress. The rumours are probably still too vague, or, more likely, he hasn't followed them up yet, and doesn't want to risk us fouling his pitch. We, on the other hand, have nothing on her in our files. No record. That's a mistake, I grant you. And now we have to work fast.' He pauses, and takes another square of chocolate.

'The morning of Fatima Rashed's murder, Bornand asks us for a personal file on Chardon. We give it to him, expurgated of course. We also know that Fatima Rashed was one of Bornand's favourite call girls and that she spent the night before she was killed at an orgy with him and his friends. Lastly, Bornand is one of Mado's main protectors, and Martenot is his lawyer. That makes too many coincidences.'

He stops and looks at them:

'Are you with me? No questions?'

She's with him.

'The scenario we're working on is the following: Chardon has something on Françoise Michel's sex life that enables him to blackmail her. It's a habit with him, and his chief source of income. He approaches Bornand, perhaps through Fatima Rashed. It ends in bloodshed. I believe Chardon's dead, otherwise he'd have contacted us to ask for protection – which we'd have given him, incidentally. Yesterday, after you left, I sent an inspector to the Brasserie des Sports. The waiter identified the one you call the second man. It's Fernandez, a cop seconded to Bornand's personal security. You see how the pieces are falling into place? And yesterday we had another new lead. Bornand's mixed up in arms trafficking in some way. So far there's nothing confirming the link with Chardon. We've decided to keep working on this hypothesis, because whatever happens, we'll get something out of it. All we need to do is find out why Chardon was blackmailing Françoise Michel, and we've got Bornand. One of my inspectors is already digging up Françoise Michel's past. The past always sheds light on the present, at least in police matters. You two will follow Françoise Michel. Pay attention to every detail, since we don't know what we're looking for.' He shoots Noria a critical look. 'Milou, will you make sure she's appropriately attired for the milieu you'll be operating in.' He opens a file lying on his desk. 'I've had a brief biography of Bornand drawn up for you, to give you an idea of the individual, plus some key dates. You may find it useful.'

FRANÇOIS BORNAND: BIOGRAPHY

Born on 10 April 1921, in Lyon, only child, family devout Catholics. Father, Raymond Bornand, career army officer. Mother, Delphine Bornand née Gautron, went to visit family in the USA in August 1939 and gave no further sign of life after the outbreak of war. François Bornand passed his baccalaureate with distinction in 1939 and enrolled in the Law faculty at Lyon university in autumn 1939. In May 1940, Captain Bornand is killed in action. François is then taken into the care of Édouard Thomas, a distant cousin of his mother's, owner and manager of the Teinturerie Lyonnaise, a dyes and chemicals factory in the Part-Dieu district of Lyon with around fifty employees. After the armistice of July '40, Thomas enters into relations with the Vichy government, the production committees and the Industrial Production Ministry. His business grows steadily until 1944 thanks to regular contracts with the German army. In January 1941, François Bornand, still a law student, joins Marshal Pétain's youth workshop, in the Allier, where he remains until October 1941. From November 1941 until November 1942, he works at Radio Vichy as a specialist youth reporter. It is alleged that he entered into contact with Resistance groups (no confirmed testimonies). He leaves Radio Vichy when the German army invades the southern zone, and returns to Lyon, to his uncle Thomas's house. He joins the collaborationist militia based in Croix-Rousse as soon as it is formed, to infiltrate it on behalf of the Resistance, according to his own account and testimonies from reliable sources gathered in 1946. He leaves it in March 1943, on the point of being unmasked, and disappears. By August 1944, he's in Paris, and takes part in the Liberation of the capital. In 1945, he meets up with Édouard Thomas who, after a bit of trouble with the Lyon Liberation Committees changes the name of his company to Thomas Chemicals and Pharmaceuticals (TCP), and establishes its head office in Paris, settling there himself and moving into the pharmaceuticals industry. In 1947, François Bornand marries Nicole Thomas, Édouard's only daughter, and the same year sets up his own import-export company specialising in trade with the emerging countries, the Middle East and Pakistan. He becomes a prominent second-hand arms dealer (reselling American stocks) and trades chemicals and pharmaceuticals, in association with his father-in-law's company. He thus acquires an in-depth knowledge of a number of foreign countries, which makes him a valuable contact for the French Intelligence Service. His political commitments support his various business activities. Pro-American and a militant anti-Communist, he eventually becomes part of the clandestine Rainbow network, financed by the CIA and set up to combat all forms of Communist penetration in France. He also maintains ongoing relations with some CIA agents in the Middle East.

In 1954, he enters into a business relationship with François Mitterrand's law firm. The two men become close on a political level, united in their opposition to the coup d'état of 13 May 1958 that restored General de Gaulle to power. From then on, Bornand distances himself from the

French secret services, while maintaining close ties with the Americans, and adopts the US position in favour of Algerian independence. Throughout the Algerian war, he maintains relations with the Provisional Government of the Algerian Republic (GPRA), chiefly business relations, which create difficulties for him in France resulting in two years' residence in Switzerland and a bigger outlet in the Middle East.

In 1963, Édouard Thomas dies of lung cancer. TCP, which has become France's fifth biggest pharmaceuticals company, is sold to Roussel, and Bornand and his wife benefit. Bornand entrusts his affairs to the Martenot law firm, his late father-in-law's lawyers. His wife leaves him the same year and moves to one of her properties in the Saumur region, where she still lives and breeds horses.

In 1965, he plays a key role in Mitterrand's presidential campaign, liaising with the major French industrialists who finance the campaign. This is his only known public appearance. He remains in the background afterwards, but is still very close to Mitterrand. In 1981, after François Mitterrand is elected, Bornand sells his import-export company, at a vastly inflated price, via the Parillaud bank, thanks to a lucky set of circumstances and the President's connections. But he holds on to some of his overseas interests, in particular in the International Bank of Lebanon (IBL) of which he is one of the founding trustees. He becomes the President's personal advisor at the Élysée where he influences foreign policy as a result of his numerous relations with the Americans, the Israelis, and with the Arab countries. He is also involved in internal security, and in this capacity plays a part in setting up and running the Elysée's 'anti-terrorist unit' in August 1982. He maintains a key role in controlling and managing this private presidential police force.

Bornand is a great womaniser; his conquests are many and fleeting. In 1966, three years after his wife left him, he meets Françoise Michel, who becomes his mistress, and still is, although without any sign of a diminution in the number of his female conquests. Furthermore, he regularly frequents prostitutes, and is on very friendly terms with Mado, France's most famous madam. He has intervened on her behalf on countless occasions when she has run into difficulties with the police, and he regularly calls on her services when he entertains foreign visitors. He is a consumer of class C drugs and some class B drugs. As far as we know, he has no problem finding suppliers and has not been threatened with blackmail.

♣

Mado snorts on entering Macquart's office.

'It's too cold for words.' The perfect bourgeois lady, as ever. Her hair is lacquered into an immaculate French pleat and her make-up discreetly minimal. She's wearing an ankle-length pearl-grey sheepskin coat and boots, and sporting a black leather Lancel handbag. Macquart waits, watching her closely, a set expression on his face. He indicates a chair. She keeps her coat on and smiles at him:

'What do you want of me, superintendent? You know that my coming here isn't exactly good publicity for my business.'

'Precisely, madame, given the nature of your business, I don't see where a police superintendent could meet you other than in his office.'

'I love your sense of humour, superintendent.'

'Good. I'm looking for Fernandez. He hasn't been seen since yesterday afternoon.'

Mado affects surprise, slightly overplayed.

'Why are you telling this to me, superintendent?'

'Because he's one of your regular customers and he's, shall we say, in business with Cecchi. I think you have more means than I do of reaching him, and he's more useful to me than he is to you. As he's done for, it's a deal where I have a lot to gain and you have little to lose. We should be able to reach an understanding.'

Silence. Mado weighs up his offer. *He knows more than I thought. Cecchi's not going to like this. After the Katryn and Chardon business, the boat is definitely letting in water.* She replies evasively:

'I'll ask my girls ...'

'I expect to hear from you today, or by tomorrow morning at the latest.' He rises to see her to the door. 'You're untouchable, Mado. But how long would you last without Cecchi? A month? Two months? Less?'

♣

As soon as the Annecy social security offices open, Laurencin is sitting facing the director. As luck would have it, a woman. But at first glance, he reckons there's no point turning on the charm. He plays the police card, Antoinette Michel is probably under threat of blackmail. 'Can you tell me what's in her file, it'll save me time and no one will be any the wiser.'

The woman takes out the file without serious protest. Born on 24 January 1926. Worker at the SNR ball bearings company in Annecy from 1946 to 1966. She draws an early retirement pension which is paid into the Leydernier bank. Never ill. And that's all. A perfectly ordinary little lady.

At the bank, Laurencin finds himself in a tiny office with a bank employee, pretending he wants to open a current account, and perhaps, depending on the terms the bank is prepared to offer, a home-buyer's savings account ... he opens the conversation. Madame Michel, his neighbour, a charming woman. He's only known her without a husband, a single woman and a very young pensioner, with no financial worries. Some people are luckier than others.

'That's for sure. With what her daughter sends her every month, she's got nothing to worry about, believe me.'

A phone call to Macquart:

'If there is blackmail going on, it seems to be the mother and daughter who've got something on Bornand.'

'Right.'

'If we cross-reference, we know that Antoinette Michel was in Lyon in 1943, that's where she gave birth to her daughter. Bornand was in Lyon, in the collaborationist Militia, the same year. A troubled time. Might be interesting to go and see what we can uncover?'

'Indeed it might.'

Mid-afternoon in Lyon. In the local archives, a charming, slightly podgy young lady, passionately interested in her work, and in attractive young lads. Laurencin weighs up the situation. *This time, turning on the charm is essential, but I already know that there'll be no surprises with her.* The pair of them bury themselves in the files, cross-referencing 1943 and Militia. And they find: Jules Michel, Antoinette's father, chief of the

Croix-Rousse Militia. And Bornand was in his group, before disappearing without trace in mid-1943.

Laurencin looks up, smiles at the librarian and buries himself once more.

September '44, Michel is killed by the partisans. In the newspapers of the day is a photo of Antoinette Michel walking forlornly down a street, her head shaven, a polka-dot dress, carrying a baby, Françoise no doubt, and a line of young men behind her, taunting her. The caption reads: 'A shorn woman, rue de Belfort.' The same street where the Michels lived, at number 29.

It is ten p.m. A cosy little dinner for two at the Brasserie Georges, the famous Lyon sausage with pistachio and a half-bottle of Brouilly. No surprises there either, but it's very pleasant. Like the wine, the librarian's lips taste of wild strawberries.

♣

The unmarked car is parked in avenue de la Bourdonnais, with the entrance to Bornand's apartment block in view. Levert is sitting behind the wheel. He laughed when Noria told him that she couldn't drive. 'What about taking photos, do you know how to do that?' No, she can't do that either. He sits doing crosswords and chewing gum. A window is wound halfway down. Noria sits stiffly beside him. Waiting, an enclosed space, proximity, a whole set of new sensations to cope with.

A white Peugeot taxi pulls up in front of the gate. Levert drops his paper and starts up the engine. Noria feels a slight contraction in her chest, the chase is on. A woman emerges, tall, slim, her camel coat belted at the waist, brown leather boots, dark brown felt hat perched on a blonde chignon, a big leather shoulder bag. Noria recognises her: the blonde she'd glimpsed at the exit to the cemetery, yesterday. Then the other person, the tall, slim guy, must have been Bornand. Noria recalls the way he grabbed her arm, pinning her to his side. The woman submitted.

The taxi pulls away. It is 15.59, she notes. Easy to follow, heavy traffic, nothing noteworthy. Arrival at the Gare de Lyon at 16.32. Françoise Michel purchases a ticket for the TGV to Geneva (and so do Ghozali and Levert), buys a pile of magazines, boards the Train Bleu and has a drink, alone. At 17.15, the train departs. Seated in first class, Françoise Michel flicks through her magazines, dozes, watches the night fly past, bored. Around 19.30, she orders a meal tray and only eats half.

Arrival in Geneva at 21.10. Taxi to the Hilton, quai du Mont-Blanc, with a view over the lake. A big, impersonal, modern luxury hotel. Françoise Michel checks in at reception and collects her key. Then she makes her way to the Lobby Bar, just behind the reception desk.

Françoise Michel makes her entrance, her bag slung over her shoulder. Noria follows her. In the meantime, Levert wanders around the shopping mall, buys a small cigar and starts to smoke it while waiting to return unobtrusively back to the lobby. Red is the colour of the carpeting, the armchairs grouped in fours around the coffee tables, the big banquettes lining the walls, the leather-covered stools, and even the big curved bar. There are soft yellow lights on the walls, spotlights embedded in the low lacquered copper ceiling, nothing intimate about the place, it looks more like a lobby fitted out between the lifts and the hotel entrance, in fairly aggressive style. Music plays in the background. In a corner, there's a piano, but it has a cover on. There are quite a lot of people in small groups, especially men, and nearly all of them seem to be talking business.

Françoise Michel hovers on the fringes of the bar area. A man gets to his feet, a fit-looking individual in his forties, with short hair and a square jaw. She makes her way over to him, with a hint of uncertainty about her movements. They exchange a few words, then he pulls out a chair for her and she sits down. *They have arranged to meet but they don't know each other*, notes Noria, close on her heels, ill at ease in these flash, pseudo-luxurious surroundings, her hand on her card wallet inside her coat pocket. She walks past the couple and sits down a few tables away, carefully choosing a corner. They order a tequila sunrise and a whisky. Noria has a herbal tea, watches and broods.

First of all a few formalities, then Françoise Michel leans towards the man over her glass, bringing her face very close to his (Noria imagines the carefully shaven skin, smooth, soft to the touch, breathes in the smell of stale tobacco. *Photo*), she wants a cigarette. The man takes a cigarette case out of his pocket and offers her one, lights it, the woman inhales deeply, studying him. She anticipates the initial contact of the two naked bodies, it will be surprise, discovery, climaxing almost instantly. Afterwards, they'll start again, more slowly, but there won't be the same thrill. She smiles at him. The man drains his glass, helps her up, takes her elbow and they leave side by side. *Photo*.

A well-paced act, skilfully executed, without any unnecessary flourishes. She's a pro, thinks Noria, slumped in her chair, letting her thoughts drift as she sips her herbal tea. Flashback to Bonfils's lips, gently defined, cool beneath her tongue. Levert threads his way slowly between the tables, joins her, sits down, crushes out his cigar in an ashtray and orders a brandy. *Cigar, cognac, what must his lips taste of right now?*

'I haven't been able to identify the man. Françoise Michel is registered under the name of Monica Davis, and they've both gone up to her room.'

'Bornand prostitutes his mistress? Macquart's scenario, with sexual blackmail thrown in, suddenly seems plausible. We must be getting close.'

'Tomorrow, we'll carry on taking photos. And now, I've booked the room next to Monica Davis for the two of us.'

Noria stiffens. Levert laughs.

'Don't start getting ideas, Ghozali. Never on duty, never with a colleague.'

Noria gets up, leans towards him and smiles:

'And never with a dirty Arab, right?'

♣

Macquart looks at his watch: nine p.m. already. Too late to go home to his large house in Chaumont-en-Vexin, surrounded by meadows. He pictures himself arriving well after ten, his wife and five children already in bed and fast asleep, nothing in the fridge, an interloper. To leave again in the morning, before they wake up … He'll have a sandwich in a brasserie around Châtelet, and spend the night in a little hotel near the Gare du Nord where they know him under the name of Durantex, a travelling sales rep.

♣

It's not hard locating Cecchi. Almost every evening, after midnight, he drops into the Perroquet Bleu club, rue Pigalle, neutral territory where the kings of the pavement meet to negotiate boundaries and tolerance zones, plus a few cops who take part in the negotiations, a handful of politicians, and a great many famous and infamous night owls seeking thrills and cocaine. Fernandez knows the place well, having been a regular at various times, initially trailing around after Bornand and then on his own account. That's where he met Cecchi. Beginning and end of a chapter.

Although Pigalle is animated at night, the narrow surrounding streets are very quiet, almost deserted. At around nine p.m., Fernandez, his nose buried in a huge bunch of gladioli, enters an apartment block in rue Henner behind a young woman who taps in the door code. He goes through to the dark courtyard, climbs over the back wall, forces open the door of a storeroom, a simple lock and two turns of the key, and finds himself in the back of a newsagent's which overlooks the Perroquet Bleu.

Fernandez puts on gloves, moving around slowly with the help of a tiny torch, gropes his way to the window and puts the gladioli and a tool belt down on the counter, within reach. He checks the time: 21.23. It'll be OK, but no time to hang around. He focuses his mind and tries to recall the exact layout of the premises on the other side of the metal shutter. He stations himself, suction disc, diamond cutter … with precise movements he cuts a big enough circle in the shop window to allow him to reach the metal shutter easily. He draws an oblong and takes out a pocket electric drill. *Don't attract attention.* He listens out and attacks just as a car drives past the shop. Don't let the drill bit go through the shutter and be visible from the street, that would be asking for trouble. He needs to be hyper aware of the intensity of the pressure and stop a second before the metal shutter gives way. His hands are skilled, his mind totally absorbed, he's sweating all over. As he makes the first holes, he gains a fuzzy picture of what's happening outside. He carries on with his painstaking task, a little less tense now. *Few pedestrians actually, the people heading for the Perroquet Bleu are all on the other side of the street.* After an hour and a half's drilling, he's cut out four-fifths of an oval. He tests the resistance of the metal with his fingertips: it gives. The satisfaction of a job well done. He puts away his equipment. Then he pushes the counter in front of the window and extracts from the bunch of gladioli a short-barrelled laser gun, borrowed from the Élysée gendarmes' armoury which always has state-of-the-art weapons. He checks the mechanism, loads it, sits on the counter and lays the gun down next to him. It is 23.38. Then begins a long wait, his eye trained on the entrance to the Perroquet Bleu.

The Perroquet Bleu. His first snort of coke, on the corner of a table. The feeling that he was discovering life. Coke, warmth, a flashback: Katryn's face, screaming, a dark hole beneath a helmet of black hair, the back of her neck split open, a bloodstain slowly spreading over the wall, her body sliding downwards in slow motion, doubled up, a heap of rags. No more sound, not now. Ghosts. A gold pill box, two amphetamines. Empty his mind, at all costs. He rehearses the sequence of actions over and over in his mind. Cecchi's car slows down and stops, Cecchi gets out, straightens up ...

At 12.16 a.m., Bornand, at the wheel of his Porsche, screeches to a halt in front of the Perroquet Bleu. Fernandez feels a jolt, an adrenalin rush. Bornand gets out and hands his keys to the doorman. Fernandez takes aim, gripped by an overwhelming urge to kill. Bornand goes inside the bar. Fernandez sighs. The adrenalin subsides. His hands are shaking. Amphetamines.

At 12.32, Cecchi's BMW arrives. He emerges from the left rear door. And from the right rear door, Beauchamp ...

Fernandez is stunned, his mind working overtime: Cecchi and Beauchamp know each other, the *Tribune de Lille*, it's them.

... They exchange a few words, laughing, over the roof of the car ...

Flandin too?

... the BMW slowly moves off and the two men walk over to the doorman and stop to greet him ...

What about the sabotaged plane? Bankrolled by arms dealers? His hand squeezes the trigger, the bullet hits Cecchi in the head. A second one shatters the neon Perroquet Bleu sign. Beauchamp and the porter fling themselves to the ground, Beauchamp, writhing in his efforts to extricate the revolver which is stuck in the folds of his coat, shoots in the direction of the metal shutter. Men come rushing out from the bar, bent double, the porter gesticulates helplessly, two or three minutes of total confusion.

Fernandez is already far away. Without waiting to check whether Cecchi was well and truly dead, he grabbed the gun and the bouquet, dashed for the door and was in rue Henner inside forty-five seconds. Within three minutes, he's melted into the crowd thronging boulevard de Clichy. He walks to place Clichy, still clutching his flowers and the concealed gun. Too late for the last metro. Above all no taxis. He disappears down the back streets between Clichy and La Fourche, at random. A black Peugeot 205, a discreet model which he knows well. One and a half minutes to pick the door lock, efficient as ever, and he drives away from the neighbourhood to the wail of police sirens coming from a few blocks away.

Wednesday 11 December

At seven a.m., Macquart, freshly showered and shaved, goes out to buy the papers at the Gare du Nord, ensconces himself at the Terminus Nord and orders a large café crème and croissants. He skims the dailies. Nothing of interest. Then picks up the *Bavard Impénitent* – the 'impenitent gossip' – the satirical weekly that comes out on Wednesdays. And there, on the front page, a short, prominently positioned article, carrying the byline of the paper's regular leader writer, André Bestégui:

The Intelligence Services aren't stool pigeons.

 Friday, 30 November, a high-class prostitute is murdered in Paris. Some customers have nasty ways. And her body is found in the vicinity of the La Villette construction site. Why not? It's as good a place to die as anywhere.

 The Crime Squad's investigating: that's their job, and on the whole they do it well. They quickly identify the last man to have seen the woman alive, a certain Chardon. Bad news. Chardon isn't just anyone. He's a gossip columnist, but that's not his only talent. He can also spice up his stories with photos of his society subjects in compromising situations, which he uses for his own ends to supplement his income. In short, most journalists earn their living by publishing, while he earns his by not publishing.

 Displaying a hopeless lack of judgement, the Crime Squad pursue their enquiries and at Chardon's home they discover a stash of Lebanese heroin that has come via French-speaking sub-Saharan Africa. Well, well, private preserve, private hunting ground, here we go again.

But that's not the end of the story: Chardon doesn't work for himself, he's in the pay of the Intelligence Service and the Paris Préfecture, who use his reports and his photos for their own ends. But the murdered prostitute worked for Mado, the madam whose clientele is made up of the rich and the powerful and has been for over a decade: politicians, businessmen, high-profile visiting dignitaries. And Mado ... as you've guessed, is on the payroll of the Paris Intelligence Service. Is this internal gang warfare within this venerable institution?

The Crime Squad would very much like to question Chardon more closely. Only the problem is, his bosses confess they have no idea where to find him. And Mado's lips are sealed.

Exit the Crime Squad, Intelligence is leading the dance.

Political police, corrupt police, a society has the police force it deserves.

Macquart swears twice, pays his bill and jumps into a taxi to get to the office as fast as possible.

There, he finds messages from Levert and Laurencin: the investigation is following its course, nothing special to report. And another from Patriat, the chief of the Crime Squad section in charge of the Fatima Rashed murder: 'Get yourself over here as soon as possible.'

Just the time to set up a meeting with the big shots from the political police in Intelligence at ten o'clock, with only one item on the agenda: the article in the *Bavard Impénitent*, and Macquart drops into his neighbours at police HQ, at 36 quai des Orfèvres.

Patriat receives him with two men from his team. Their expressions are weary and drawn.

'It's been a tough night. Cecchi was killed at around half past midnight, outside the Perroquet Bleu …'

Macquart doesn't need to feign surprise.

'… my team was very grateful for your assistance over Chardon.' Patriat pauses. 'Mado accuses you of being behind the murder. Apparently you summoned her to your office yesterday and allegedly threatened her by saying she wouldn't last a month if Cecchi were killed.'

'Likely story.'

The first meeting of the day in Macquart's office is somewhat gloomy. The general feeling is that Bestégui's article is remote-controlled by Bornand; everyone knows of the connection between the two men.

'It's Bornand's declaration of war on the Intelligence Service.'

'It looks like it.'

'And do you have any idea why, over and above his visceral hatred for all the official police departments?'

'No, not really. The fact that Chardon's on our payroll doesn't seem a strong enough reason. And we weren't the ones to open hostilities …'

'An attack on Mado in the same article is a first in this kind of paper, which has always gone easy on her … After all, the journalists use the same sources as we do …'

'The same day as her man gets a bullet through the brain. Does that seem like a coincidence?'

'Who shot him?'

'No idea.'

'Something to do with taking control of the Bois de Boulogne gambling club maybe?'

'It's always possible, but we haven't heard a thing.'

'In any case, we didn't put a bullet in his brain, but the accusations against Mado … that's a very crafty move. If it's war, it's possible that Bornand's hand is behind them in an attempt to drive her out. And that is going to make our case massively harder going.'

'And it's also possible that Bornand's behind Cecchi's murder too, why not? He's capable of it. Could Fernandez be involved?'

Macquart responds to the barrage of questions. 'I've got people out looking for him, I still think he's our best bet. But no sign of him. He appears to have vanished into thin air, like Chardon. That's a lot of disappearances.' A silence. 'Right, I need to take a step back and try and fathom this out. I'm waiting for news from my team. No need to give up hope, or to rush into things. Shall we go and have a sauerkraut at L'Alsace à Paris, along with a decent bottle of wine?'

♣

Françoise Michel comes down at 09.17, still accompanied by the same man. *Photo.* (This time it's Levert who has the camera.) They pay for their rooms, then leave on foot, taking the lakeside road. She's carrying her big shoulder bag. She takes his arm and they walk fast. The weather is sunny and cold, with Mont Blanc clearly visible above the lake.

At 09.37, they enter the Occidentale des Banques Suisses building. They come out again at 10.25 with two suitcases. *Photo.* At 10.32, barely five minutes' further on, they walk into the Banque Commerciale de Genève. *Photo.* A wait. Then they come out again at 11.40, without the suitcases. He's carrying a leather briefcase. *Photo.* Two taxis are waiting for them.

The cops follow that of Françoise Michel to Cornavin Station where she boards the TGV for Paris at 12.15.

On arrival at the Gare de Lyon, and while Noria watches Françoise Michel in the taxi queue, Levert telephones Macquart.

'Drop it for now, we know where to find her. Come back to my office straight away, with your photos.'

'Move it, Ghozali. We're letting her go, Macquart's waiting for us, no time even for a sandwich.'

In Macquart's office, Levert, Noria and the three superintendents study the photos spread out in front of them. The ones taken by Noria first. Clumsily framed and a bit fuzzy. 'You'll have to learn,' was Macquart's only terse comment. Then the others, taken by Levert, that morning, in the street outside the banks. These are unarguably clear.

'Without a shadow of a doubt, that's Moricet. Well known to the police, as they say.'

'Formerly of the Élysée special unit and the secret services.'

'A security mercenary who works for the Saudis.'

'I've heard that he's also closely linked to the Syrians.'

'Yes, them too. He's not proud.'

'A killer. Wanted for murder in several countries.'

'But not in France.'

'In any case, a big fish,' concludes Macquart. 'With a man of his ilk in the picture, as well as the suitcase probably stuffed with dosh, and the *Tribune* article, this clearly puts matters in a different league from Chardon's little schemes.'

Everyone sits up. Macquart seems mentally elsewhere.

'It all comes back to arms trafficking. And that's not necessarily good news for us. We're not in charge of that side of things.'

After accompanying his companion of the previous night to the municipal archive Laurencin, clearly not sorry to part company, heads for rue de Belfort, in a working-class district. Naturally, at number 29, there's no trace of the Michel family, and the current owners have no recollection of them. Laurencin sets off on a tour of the shops. Bakery-cum-patisserie, a cheese seller, a butcher, but none of them had been there during the war years. He grabs a sandwich and a beer.

At the end of the street is a hardware shop. Laurencin pushes open the door, setting off an irritatingly shrill bell. The shop is long and narrow, dark, apparently containing a workshop at the back, from which comes the sound of a hacksaw and the smell of burnt iron. Floor-to-ceiling shelving, massive counters propped across chests of drawers in the middle of the room, and just about everything everywhere. Tins of nails, screws, nuts, washers, spanners, tools, taps, watering cans, casserole dishes, stepladders, planters. Hanging from the ceiling, amid the brooms, are feather dusters, real ones, with real feathers, and a bunch of leather straps. Laurencin wants to touch everything, he feels as though he's stepped into the dream childhood he never had. An old man makes his way towards him from the back of the shop, all smiles, wearing a grey dust-jacket, a beret and safety boots. Laurencin bangs his right hand on a corner of the counter to make sure he's not dreaming.

They exchange formalities, then Laurencin says:

'I'm trying to find out what happened to a certain Michel who lived at number 29 during the war, and his daughter Antoinette.'

'The name doesn't ring a bell, but you know, I was a prisoner of war for five years, and then, in '45, I left for Australia ...'

Laurencin glances around: 'Australia ...'

'Oh yes, I was a cowboy for several years, then I came and settled here, with my wife, who's Australian. Does that surprise you?'

'Depress me, you mean. If you can't tell me about the Michels, who in this neighbourhood can?'

'Doctor Méchin, at number 35. He took over his father's practice, years ago now, and he's never left rue de Belfort. If anyone remembers your Michel, it'll be him.'

Laurencin thanks him and goes back up the street, finds number 35 and Doctor Méchin's surgery. The waiting room's crowded, he has a spot of bother with the practice secretary. The doctor won't be free until early evening. 'Let's say at around seven o'clock, at the Café de Belfort just down the road.' Several hours to kill. Laurencin goes back to the hardware store for a chat with the veteran cowboy.

♣

At Security headquarters, Macquart is given a warm reception by Superintendent Lanteri, who is very interested in the photos of Moricet and the names of the banks visited by Françoise Michel. He reveals a few nuggets of information in exchange. They'd found papers on Cecchi implicating Bornand directly in the Iranian arms deal, an operation for which the SEA was seemingly merely a cover. (Any connection with the suitcases full of notes? Possible, but not obvious, it still remained to be proved.) Bornand, who was at the Perroquet Bleu at the time of the murder, had been questioned in this office, that very morning. For the moment, it is officially recognised that those papers were false, and that Cecchi had been planning to use them to blackmail Bornand. Cecchi's stool pigeon, a certain Beauchamp, head of security at the SEA, has been arrested. He's a friend of Chardon's. It's possible that he's mixed up in Cecchi's murder.

'It's a very complicated case, involving a great many people – potential dynamite.' Lanteri taps the table with his finger-tips. 'And we're in sole charge of it.'

Macquart nods and waits. Lanteri goes on: 'For reasons that escape me, Bornand seriously has it in for the Paris Intelligence department.'

'I read the article in the *Bavard Impénitent*.'

'So did I, but that's not all. After leaving here, Bornand went to the Interior Ministry where he used all his influence to push for the disbanding of the Intelligence Service again.' Another pause. 'If the Iranian arms case is closed, if he recovers his full freedom to manoeuvre, he can cause you real damage.'

'And will he recover it?'

'It certainly looks that way. The plane vanished in thin air, Flandin dead of a heart attack, Cecchi murdered. What about Beauchamp, do you know him?' Macquart nods. 'He's ready to bargain anything for his freedom and a new start in life ... He was associated with Bornand in the past, and probably holds quite a few trumps.' Lanteri sighs. Bornand's one of those people who are indestructible. Always ready to bounce back.

Macquart goes back to Intelligence headquarters, to get on with some dreary routine paperwork. In a corner, Levert and Noria are writing their reports and filing the photos.

Still no news from Laurencin. Macquart gets a coffee from the machine and eats two chocolates. *Got to nab Bornand as quickly as possible, it's him or us. What do I have left? Fernandez, if he's still alive, if I can find him. Chancy. And the names of the Swiss banks. Given the Security department's position, for the time being, the only way to use this information is an anonymous letter. But who to send it to? Not to the* Bavard. *Too close to Bornand and they wouldn't publish it, or not soon enough. To the magistrate investigating Cecchi's killing? It depends who's in charge of the case, and besides, the prosecutor may well refuse to delay the hearing. No obvious link with Cecchi's murder. And no other investigations running. Switzerland? That might be a good idea, Switzerland …*

⚜

The pair of them are sitting at a small round table. Laurencin has ordered a coffee and the waiter brings the doctor half a bottle of Beaujolais without being asked.

'Why are you interested in the Michel family?'

He knows them. Think carefully.

'I'm a historian. I specialise in the war years and the Liberation in Lyon. I've found some unsigned personal documents on this period, and I'm having trouble seeing how they fit in. They contain quite a lot of references to Michel and his daughter Antoinette, and I'm trying to cross-reference …'

It'll have to do, for a hasty explanation …

'Do you know if Antoinette's still alive, doctor?'

'I have no idea. I haven't seen a death certificate with her name on it in Lyon, but she could have moved away, abroad, perhaps.'

Laurencin looks at the doctor. *I'm on the right track, he wants to talk. Mustn't rush him.* He allows a long silence to set in, then Méchin speaks:

'It is a painful memory for me.' He breaks off. 'Michel was a brute who used to beat his wife. According to my father, he beat her to death. But that was during the war, he was in the Militia and nobody asked any questions. He also used to beat his daughter, Antoinette. She got pregnant, she was very young. I don't remember the date …'

'Her daughter was born in October '43.'

'Sounds possible. It was my father who told Michel the news, and who took the girl into our house for a while, to protect her from being beaten. And then, on the Liberation, Michel was killed in his apartment, nobody was sorry, but it happened in front of his daughter, it wasn't a pretty business, and afterwards her head was shorn and she was paraded around the whole city.' He stops. 'And this is the really painful part. My father took care of Antoinette, he knew the child's father, but he hadn't really been part of the Resistance, he was afraid, and he didn't lift a finger to defend her, and neither did I. And she was never seen again. Forty years on, and it's still something I'm not exactly proud of.'

'Who was the father? Wasn't he around either?'

'A young militiaman who spent a lot of time with Michel. His name was Bornand.' Laurencin found it hard not to show his surprise. 'He disappeared during Antoinette's pregnancy and we never saw him again. He must have been killed. You know, a lot of people got killed during those years.'

'Well, that answers my question. The author of my documents must be this person, Bornand.'

Macquart takes Laurencin's call at eight p.m. Françoise Michel is Bornand's daughter.

'Come back to Paris right away, Laurencin.' A silence. 'And thank you.'

Noria and Levert look up from their work. Macquart looks back at them and smiles. Incredible. A broad, jubilant smile through set lips, not exactly reassuring.

'You see, these are rare moments of triumph. We were mistaken, not completely, but almost completely, and we're going to win all the same. I don't know what comes closer than this to pure happiness.'

The phone rings. Macquart picks up the receiver. 'It's Fernandez on the line,' says the switchboard operator. Fernandez ... well, well, good things always come in threes.

'Can you trace the call?'

'We're already onto it, superintendent.'

'Good. Put him through ... Hello, Fernandez.'

'Superintendent, I'd like to talk to you, can I come in and see you?'

'Spot of trouble, young man?'

'Yes, superintendent, big trouble.'

Bornand's envoy? I don't think so, not now, when Bornand thinks he's holding all the aces, and not after having gone underground for forty-eight hours. But I've got a better card. I'll keep it back for now. Just in case ... I've got Bornand in a stranglehold, and it won't take him long to realise it.

'I'm up to my ears, Fernandez. Come and see me on Friday, does that suit you?'

'Perfect, thank you, superintendent.'

Macquart hangs up. The switchboard calls back: Hôtel de la République, in Saint-Germain-en-Laye. Where he's been staying since last Monday.

Macquart addresses Noria and Levert:

'You're off to Saint-Germain. It's close to Paris, and rather a pleasant place. You're going to find out what Fernandez wants to tell us, since he doesn't appear to have taken any precautions to stop us tracing his call. And be back here as soon as you can. Tomorrow morning, I'm the one who'll have the duty and honour of informing the President of the delicate situation in which his advisor finds himself …'

Thursday 12 December

At the Intelligence Service headquarters there was tension in the air as the day dragged by following Macquart's return from the Élysée. Eyes and ears had been positioned everywhere they possibly could. Reports came in regularly: nothing's happening. Bornand is at home, he's not moving, not telephoning, not receiving any visitors. Françoise Michel is having dinner with a girlfriend at the Champs Élysées Drugstore as if it were the most normal thing in the world. They're going to the cinema to see *The Year of the Dragon*. Macquart wagers she has no idea of what's going on.

Fernandez arrived at the Hôtel de la République, in Saint-Germain-en-Laye at around midnight on Monday evening. He parked his car in a paying car park, and hasn't moved it since. He goes for walks in the forest, reads the newspaper, bets on the horses and plays table football at the nearest bar-cum-tobacconist and betting shop, eats at the hotel and drinks whisky in his room.

Macquart summarises for them. 'In other words, he's telling us that he's been out of Paris since Monday evening. But he's right next to a busy train station where there's no likelihood of his being identified … We'll soon see about that.'

♣

Bornand has shut himself up in his drawing room and sits slumped in an armchair. He's had his mistress informed that he's not available, sent Antoine away, locked his door, unplugged the telephone, and opened a bottle of vodka. The President refused to see him and congratulated himself in front of his closest associates for never having invited Françoise Michel to the Élysée. The verdict has been delivered and it is final: no scandals of this nature in the corridors of the presidential palace. Bornand is asked to leave his office at the Élysée immediately, and its door is now closed to him. With all his files inside. He is not the only one who understands the workings of power. He is to put an immediate end to this affair, and ostensibly go back to living with his wife. 'Then, we'll see,' says the President, 'it all depends on the reaction of the press and of public opinion.'

Bornand takes a large slug of vodka and closes his eyes. Go back to living with his wife. A half smile. They never had lived together. They'd lived in the same house while Thomas was alive, that's all that can be said. Then Bornand's wife moved away to live in Saumur, one day after the funeral. It was several days before he noticed she'd gone. So, resume their cohabitation, why not?

The vodka bottle is empty. His stomach's burning. He feels shut in. Plagued, as in the past. Sees himself locked in his room with Thomas, his father-in-law to be, pacing the floor, shouting, randomly banging into furniture.

'In the Militia! You idiot … What are you trying to do? Act the martyr? … Wake up. This is March 1943. The Germans have lost Stalingrad, the Americans are in North Africa and the Japanese are retreating in the Pacific. Can't you see for yourself that Hitler has lost the war, and Vichy and the Militia will go down with him?'

He follows Thomas with his eyes and says nothing. Vichy, the new homeland, building the Europe of tomorrow, destroying Communism, the enemy of Western civilisation, is he the only person who believes in it?

'The kids' games are over. You'll go and live with my mother in the country, and you stay put until further orders. Let people forget you. I'll have enough on my plate trying to salvage my business after the war, without having a collaborator on my hands as well.'

He gave in, that's all, neither a rebel nor a hero. Just like today. The solitude is unbearable. Of course he will step back in line and go back to his wife, at least for a while. He opens another bottle of vodka and falls asleep.

Friday 13 December

Bornand wakes up in a daze. *Blood spurting in the telephone booth, strangers, their faces pressed to the glass, staring at him in curiosity, revulsion? He's covered in blood.* He gets up with difficulty, picks up a pretty Chinese lacquer box from the table behind the sofa and snorts two pinches of cocaine. Lies down again and breathes slowly, his eyes closed.

Dead. A man of around forty, who looks like an ordinary kind of man, a primary school teacher, three streets away from the Michel's place, and a Communist before the war. 'A man who supports the Resistance,' said Michel. Five of them lay in wait for him, with coshes, under a porch on a street corner. In broad daylight. When he came out, they jumped on him. Bornand got him in the shoulder, he fell to his knees, more blows and he keeled over exposing the nape of his neck, and Bornand struck. A sound of snapping wood and the Communist's body lay motionless on the ground. A few more kicks, to let off steam. Intense. No comparison with Flandin's abstract murder. They return, accomplices and victors both. Then Thomas locks him in his bedroom. End of story.

He has always been attracted by killers. Flashback to Moricet walking through the streets of Beirut, his gun wedged into his belt in the small of his back, under his elegantly cut jacket. Killers with class. Even Cecchi … A lot of deaths recently. Karim … hardly a murder, more a vanishing shadow. Flandin, Cecchi … Cecchi whose corpse flashes into his mind, half his face blown away, on the pavement outside the Perroquet Bleu …

No doubt a gangland killing, even if I let Mado think I believe the Intelligence Service had him killed. In any case, his death came at an opportune moment, ridding me of a burdensome ally. I have to admit that in the end he had me completely at his mercy. This murder is a stroke of luck. Of course.

He gets up and sits down on the sofa, runs his hand through his hair and smoothes his moustache. The President also has his family secrets, and is very keen for them to remain secret. *I am the man who knows. He can't manage without me. I just need to lie low for a few days at my wife's house, and I'll be back.*

He gets up and goes into the bathroom. A freezing shower and a handful of amphetamines to keep himself awake.

What do I do with Françoise? When she came to my place, the first time, blackmail and seduction, a real gift out of the blue. I fucked her and flaunted her. So, incest, it's just a word. You get used to it, you get bored, as with everything else. Don't want to fuck any more. Flashback to the blonde fury, the other day. I'm losing her. Almost relieved to leave her without a confrontation. When things have calmed down, I'll set her up in a furnished apartment with an allowance. She'll understand. She has no choice.

He gets into his Porsche, and drives alongside the Seine towards the west of Paris.

He is tailed by two cars from Intelligence. Departure 05.07. Erratic driving. Pont de Sèvres, 05.30, then he takes the N118. All good, he's on his way. He accelerates suddenly, they lose him. *Presumably he's heading for Saumur, we'll take the A10 motorway.* Back on Bornand's trail at the first service station.

He fills up. The car is parked in front of the shop. Bornand buys razors, shaving foam. He goes into the toilets and shuts himself in a stall. Makes himself vomit. Then, standing bare-chested at the washbasins, he splashes himself with water, washes his face, rinses out his mouth and has a shave. Peering into the mirror, he is tense and on his guard. He trims his moustache with the razor and combs his hair. He goes into the shop, eats a sandwich, drinks three coffees, swallows two pills and gets back onto the motorway at 06.15. He drives at a steady, moderate speed. They have no difficulty keeping him in sight.

Another stop at Le Mans, where he calls his wife to announce his arrival. It is 07.45.

❧

This is the chance Macquart's been waiting for.

'Ghozali, go and see Françoise Michel. She knows about Bornand's business deals, we had proof of that in Geneva. Find a way of getting her to tell you all she knows. Woman to woman … I'm counting on you …'

He leaves the words hanging in the air.

❧

On reaching the outskirts of Saumur, Bornand vaguely remembers having been there before when his wife bought the estate, but he gets lost. He asks the way, crosses the whole centre of Saumur, follows the Loire, drives up along the cliff and takes a dirt road between two big paddocks where the horses graze. At 08.50 he parks his car in a gravelled courtyard in front of a small eighteenth-century manor house built of white limestone with a blue slate roof. The front door opens into a hall that runs through the house and leads out via a French window to the terrace and the grounds. A man in his forties wearing brown velvet trousers and a heavy beige polo-neck sweater, greets him.

'Madame Bornand is finishing off her inspection of the stables.'

Madame Bornand. He knew, of course, that she had kept her married name, but hearing it, today and in this house …

'I'll wait for her.'

He is shown into a sort of parlour, a small room adjoining the kitchen, all in white limestone, with a chequered white stone and slate floor, a tall narrow fireplace where a log fire burns lazily, a worn leather armchair in front of the fire, a big oak farmhouse table and a few straw-bottomed chairs. In a corner near the fireplace is a coat rack heaped with old rain-coats, hats and leather chaps. There's a smell of wet earth and horses. He goes over to the French window. In front of him is the end of the terrace, then a vast tree-fringed manicured lawn stretching down to the stables below. He puts a log on the fire, pokes it, then returns to the window. Facing him is a sandy avenue leading directly to the far end of the estate. She'll come up this path to meet him. His mind goes back to an image of himself standing in the chancel of the church of Saint-Pierre-de-Chaillot, aged twenty-four, wearing morning dress. The church is packed out, there are probably hymns and organ music, but he can't hear anything. He stares at the red carpet stretching straight ahead of him to the open porch, and in the pool of light, a couple is walking towards him. Thomas, a dashing fifty-something, very slim in his grey morning coat, his daughter on his arm, in her wedding dress, slowly approaching. Thomas watches him intently, only him, smiling.

He stops in front of him, places his hand on his shoulder, Bornand closes his eyes. When he opens them again, the girl is now alone beside him, her face concealed by the white tulle veil. What did she look like that day? Impossible to remember. And today, what will she look like? A woman without a face.

He shudders. Nothing stirs in the park outside. He goes back to the fire and sinks into the armchair, resting the back of his neck against the leather, his eyes half closed. A few images, the moving curve of a very long, pear-shaped breast, dense pubic hair, the warmth of an armpit, but no face. From the catalogue of his mistresses, not a single face emerges. Even that of Françoise, always overcast by the ghost of her adolescent mother's face, is hazy, uncertain. *For me, women have been no more than territories where I've met men, men with whom I've made peace or war, men whom I've loved or fought, which amounts to the same thing*, he thinks half dreaming.

Christine Bornand comes in through the kitchen door. He jumps. He must have dozed off. He looks at her with curiosity. Not very tall, a bit plump, a lively woman with short, curly chestnut hair, hazel eyes and chubby cheeks, pink from the cold. *She's about the same age as me and not a wrinkle.* He gets to his feet, she gives him a cold stare, then begins to remove her anorak and leather chaps. The man who showed Bornand in brings a tray from the kitchen with two china cups, a big coffee pot and a basket full of little pastries, puts it down on the table and leaves the room. Christine Bornand sits down and motions him to do likewise.

'Coffee, is that all right with you? So to what do I owe this visit? I worked out that we haven't seen each other for twenty-two years, not since my father's death. Twenty-two years, exactly the age of the first brood mare that was born here. She didn't get pregnant this year.'

She bites into a *pain au chocolat*.

He finds it very hard to approach her. Even though he prepared for this meeting, he's not on top form as a result of the vodka and amphetamines.

'I'm in a very nasty mess.' Christine dithers, then takes a second *pain au chocolat*. 'I got dragged into a deal selling arms to Iran that was borderline legal and which, for the time being, is costing me a fortune ...' *not good, cut to the chase, you can see she doesn't give a fuck* ... 'worst of all it's likely to get me into trouble with the law. Until the storm dies down, I've got to appear exemplary. But I'm not, and I never have been.' *Bite the bullet and get it over with quickly.* 'The woman who lives with me, or, to be more precise, in the apartment above mine, is my daughter ...'

Christine knocks her coffee over onto her trousers, scalds herself, and groans.

'... That has led to all sorts of rumours, unfounded of course. But I have to put an end to them. I've come to ask you if I might possibly come and stay here, or if you would accompany me to Paris, and live in my apartment for a few months.'

The telephone rings. Christine gets up, goes into the hall and picks it up. She calls:

'François, it's for you ... have you already given your secretary my number?'

When he picks up the receiver, the caller hangs up. *Françoise, without a doubt. Who else? She already knows? Who told her? I'll sort that out when I get back.*

Christine has poured herself another coffee and is smiling at him.

'I don't want to hear another word about that girl. You have no idea how delighted I am to learn you're in the shit. How could you imagine for one moment that I would lift a finger to help you?'

'We're still married …'

'We have never been married, François. You didn't marry me, you were adopted by my father. Two very different things.'

Irritated, Bornand adds:

'I meant we're still legally married, and with a shared inheritance which your father insisted upon. Which means that this estate, for example, is as much mine as it is yours. Which means that we had better come to some agreement and support each other.'

He speaks in an assured, frankly menacing tone. Christine rubs her hand mechanically over her coffee-stained trousers. She remains silent for a long time, gazing at the fire. Then she gets up:

'Wait here for me, I'm going to get changed.'

Once the door closes behind her, Bornand goes to sit in the old armchair and lets himself go, his body slumped, his eyes closed. *Is it possible that I've won, once again?* He feels a sort of numb indifference.

♣

Noria rings the ground-floor bell of Bornand's apartment. A man opens the door.

'Police. I'd like to speak to Françoise Michel.'

He shows her into the drawing room, quite coolly, without offering to take her coat, and leaves her there without saying a word.

Noria walks around the room, fingering her card wallet. She feels so fundamentally foreign to the scenes of Venetian life that they make her want to laugh. Her intuition is to emphasise the difference between them, and so enhance her sense of superiority and safety. She pictures Bornand again, at the cemetery gate, pinning Françoise Michel to his side with a violent movement, which she accepted. *I'm the stronger one.*

Françoise Michel comes in, wearing a chunky white Arran sweater. You really have to be skinny to wear one of those. Noria looks at her with curiosity. *She's got class. I haven't.*

'Antoine tells me you're from the police …'

'Officer Ghozali, Intelligence, Paris.'

Noria shows her ID.

'What do you want of me?'

'I have been asked to give you some information about an ongoing investigation which concerns you directly.'

Françoise Michel remains ostentatiously standing, propped against the mantelpiece.

'I'm listening. Make it quick, please.'

Noria leans against the back of the sofa, to give an impression of composure, seems to falter, then takes the plunge:

'The President was informed yesterday that you are Bornand's daughter.'

Françoise Michel starts. *Good point, I'm ahead, Macquart was right.*

'And what has my relationship with Bornand got to do with you?'

'Me personally, absolutely nothing, but apparently, the President is not of the same opinion.'

'What does he know of our private life? Nothing. And there's nothing to know. We're not married, as far as I know.'

'That is not his view at all. He considers that a scandal among his entourage would be very damaging, with the elections coming up in March '86, in a country which, as you know, still has a strong Catholic tradition and in which people take a dim view of incest.'

'Who says we sleep together?'

'Nobody. And I repeat that I don't care. But Bornand didn't react in the same way as you.' *She's wavering. Go for it.* 'The President insisted on his going back home to live with his wife. To which he agreed.'

'I don't believe a word of it.'

Bingo. I've got her.

'As you wish. He arrived at his wife's place in Saumur at 08.50 this morning. And he's still there.'

Shock. She hesitates, staring intently at Noria. Then she strides resolutely over to the telephone sitting on an occasional table, looks up a number in an address book and dials.

'Hello … May I speak to François Bornand, please …'

'One moment …' A woman's voice dripping with irony, at some distance from the phone. 'François, it's for you. Have you already given your secretary my number?'

She hangs up, ashen-faced, unplugs the telephone and goes over to sit on the sofa. *Concentrate, she's mine.* Noria takes off her coat and lays it on the wooden seat. Then she settles in one of the armchairs. Françoise doesn't have the energy to protest.

'What do you want from me? You haven't come here just to tell me I've been dumped?'

'No, I haven't …'

Noria takes a set of black and white photos out of the back pocket of her trousers, and lays them on the coffee table. Françoise Michel and Moricet, easily recognisable, in Geneva, in the lobby of the Hilton, in the street, outside the banks … She spreads them out and contemplates them. *I swear she's afraid.*

'… I'm afraid you may not be aware of who the man beside you is …'

Françoise Michel loses track for a second. *A disappointing night, once the initial excitement was over. As is often the case. Rough and ready virility …* She turns her attention back to Noria, who adds:

'… Moricet, a French mercenary based in Lebanon, wanted by the police in several countries for murder. You're the one giving him money, are you aware what that means? Money that we can easily trace, since we have the date the deposit was made and the name of the bank. Money which we assume is of criminal origin, arms trafficking, corruption, and murder. You are an accomplice.'

Françoise Michel, huddled on the sofa, says nothing. She stares at this girl who looks so young, she could be anyone, with such an ordinary face, and suddenly, such power … *I'm honestly afraid I'm no match for her.* She picks up the photos, slowly inspects them, trying to buy time to muster her thoughts.

'Was it you who followed me to Geneva?'

'Yes.' Becoming aggressive: 'I saw you getting picked up by a stranger.'

Shocked, Françoise Michel rises: 'Thank you for all this information, which I shall try to make good use of. I'll see you out.'

Noria doesn't move.

'I wouldn't play that game if I were you. You don't seem to realise the gravity of your situation. Well I'm going to tell you. You're in big trouble, very big trouble. Accomplice to a murderer, accomplice to the misuse of company property and to money laundering. That's not all. You're going to be crucified by the press as a perverse seductress, and it won't be long before you're accused of having blackmailed poor Bornand, with all that money you regularly pay into your mother's account. You'd do better to listen to what I have to say to you.'

Françoise Michel sits down again. Cornered. Then, after a silence:

'I'm listening.'

'Bornand's ditched you, and he's finished. You must leave here. Look out for yourself and your mother and salvage what there still is to be salvaged.'

'Meaning what?'

'Cooperate with the police. We want to know about Bornand's business dealings, his bank accounts, his friends and his foibles. And we think you can help us. We'll find out everything we need to know in the end, with or without your help, but it will take time, and to move fast, we need you.'

'And?'

'And you remain free, we play down your involvement, we protect your private life as far as possible. That's already quite a lot. It means you have a chance of coming out of this without being completely broken and ruined.'

'Are you asking me to betray Bornand?'

Noria leans forward, on the tip of her tongue the words to evoke the beatings, her own mother's moans as she lay on the kitchen floor, her father dazed, the fraction of a second of nothingness, desertion and deliverance. And with a sudden warmth:

'Madame, for women, freedom often begins with a betrayal. Believe me, I know what I'm talking about.'

'You're unusually sincere for a cop.'

She's going to come round. Give her time. Noria stands up, turns towards the fireplace, and contemplates the snake goddess.

Françoise Michel retreats further into the back of the sofa, her eyes closed. She feels like vomiting. Dumped, just like that. He jumps into his Porsche, and takes off. Not a word, and goes back to his wife. Dumped after twenty years' submission and dependence. *What you want doesn't count.* Dumped, like her mother, in the middle of the war, and pregnant. And she feels that knot of rage form in her belly and rise to her throat with a vengeance. Fury, hatred, the blows, Martenot on the floor, doing nothing to defend himself. *I am that woman too, even if I try to forget it.* She stares at Noria's back; the young female cop is still absorbed in studying the snake goddess. *And at this precise moment, I hate Bornand. Freedom begins with betrayal.* She sits up.

'Men are always full of surprises, don't you think?' Noria turns around. 'And they're reckless. I'm prepared to tell you everything I know.'

'Not here. I'll accompany you to the station to make an official statement.'

In the street, Levert is waiting at the wheel of an Intelligence Service vehicle. Françoise Michel climbs into the back, and Noria the front. There is a heavy silence. Levert concentrates on driving the car, Françoise Michel, gutted, mulls over her loathings and her woes, and Noria looks out at the city speeding past, no pedestrians about, the traffic is moving freely. They head for the city centre along the left bank, crossing the Seine at Les Invalides. A grey light. The darker mass of the glass roof of the Grand Palais, the Seine, vaguely luminescent, no wind, barely any movement of the water as a barge passes.

It's in the bag.

When you take the time to look, this city is wonderfully tranquil. Macquart's words echo: *I don't know what comes closer than this to pure happiness* ...

♣

The door opens and Bornand turns around. Just in time to say to himself: a very elegant trouser suit, navy blue with white stripes, Yves Saint Laurent no doubt, looks good on all women, even the plump ones. She's pointing a twelve-bore double-barrelled shotgun at him, buckshot cartridges dangling from a tungsten wire. She shoots twice, in quick succession, aiming for his chest. She hits him in the heart, Bornand is almost split in two: death is instantaneous. She stares at the pool of blood spreading on the black and white flagstones. The local stone is porous. It'll have to be sanded to get rid of the bloodstains, maybe it'll even be necessary to replace several flagstones. The opposite wall is also spattered. She sighs. Lays the hot gun on the table, next to the coffee cups. The smell of burnt gunpowder is stronger than that of horses, stronger than that of blood. Then she walks over to the telephone in the hall and dials the number of the local police.

'Good morning, chief, Madame Bornand speaking.'

'Good morning to you. madame. Has one of your horses bolted again?'

'No, chief. You'll have to come up to the stables. I've just killed my husband.'

Fernandez waits in a poky, windowless office, more of a cubby-hole than an office to be honest. Two chairs, a table, a standard lamp. A padded door. The sounds of the building barely filter through. A cross-examination room. Conditioning. He goes over and over what he will and won't say. *Yes, Katryn. If Cecchi knew, Macquart is also likely to know. An unfortunate accident. Nothing about Chardon, since nobody suspects me. Yes, everything I know about Bornand, including Flandin's death. Nothing about Cecchi's killing, I have an alibi.*

He's already been waiting two hours when Macquart comes in, places a transistor on the table and sits down. He exudes a sort of tight lipped inner jubilation. *Never seen him like that before. He's scary.* Fernandez clears his throat.

'I've come to ask you if I can be transferred back to my original department.'

Macquart looks at him, on the verge of a smile.

'So the life of a bent cop's hell, is it?'

Fernandez doesn't respond. Macquart continues:

'There's an entrance fee.'

'I'm prepared to pay it.'

'I'm going to come clean with you. I know a lot of things. I'm going to let you talk. If you tell me what I want to hear, I'll do everything within my power to take you back. If you don't, I'll have you charged. I've got what I need to do so. Deal?'

'Deal.'

'Let's go.'

Fernandez begins to speak. The plane crash, Chardon and the Iranian arms deal dossier …

'How did Bornand get hold of it?'

'Through Bestégui, from the *Bavard Impénitent* ... Katryn as a possible source ... Her death, my fault, a cock-up, Bornand doesn't know ... After that, Bornand contacts Beauchamp to get him to watch Flandin ... He hushes up the dossier ... which reappears on Monday, I don't know how, and eliminates Flandin in front of me, at Laurent's. I still don't know how. Probably with Beauchamp's help. I didn't see a thing.'

'It's not very hard to murder cleanly when you know there'll be no autopsy and no inquest ...'

'Yes, but Bornand a killer, things were getting too heavy for me and I panicked. I went into hiding that evening in a hotel in Saint-Germain-en-Laye, where I'd stayed in happier times, and where I called you from. And I stayed there until today. I think that's all.'

Macquart leans towards him:

'Is that really all?'

'I think so.'

'Cecchi was murdered forty-eight hours ago.'

'I know, I saw it on TV.'

'In the inside pocket of his jacket, the Crime Squad found a handwritten document describing the entire financial workings of the Iran missiles deal. It would appear that the SEA is just a front to buy the missiles from the armaments division of the Defence Ministry and transfer the sales commissions. But the initial outlay, five million francs, and the guarantee of three and a half million were paid by the SAPA to the IBL, Bornand's Lebanese bank which is covering the entire operation. And it's the SAPA that will receive most of the anticipated profits, i.e. around thirty million francs. If we deduct twenty per cent for the commissions, that still makes a tidy little profit of over twenty million. Now the SAPA belongs to one man, and that is Bornand. Did you know that?'

'No.' After a pause: 'Bornand always talks about France's interests in Iran, and never about his own.'

'And you truly believe he's capable of distinguishing between the two? This is hardly new.'

Macquart stops and looks at Fernandez who doesn't need to pretend he's at a loss. He allows him a breather and continues:

'Obviously, a presidential advisor who speculates privately on clandestine arms trafficking with Iran, and who pockets such huge sums is bound to make waves.' Macquart adopts an aggressive tone: 'You thought you were being clever, but you were nothing but a minnow in a sea of sharks. You were their stooge.' A pause. 'I'll continue. Cecchi was intending to blackmail Bornand. He met the journalist from the *Tribune de Lille* and dug up the Chardon dossier last Monday, by way of a warning shot. And he had an appointment with Bornand at the Perroquet Bleu to offer him a deal. What deal?'

'Maybe the re-opening of the Bois de Boulogne gambling club. He was set on it, and Bornand didn't want to touch it.'

'Cecchi got hold of the Chardon dossier from *Combat Présent*. It was Tardivel who gave it to him.' In his mind's eye, Fernandez sees Tardivel's head lolling backwards, his glasses flying off, his vision blurred. It must have been even worse with Cecchi. 'It remains to be seen how he obtained the information he was carrying on his person when he was shot. None of it seemed to appear in the Chardon dossier. Do you have any suggestions?'

'No.' *Way out of my depth, and have been from the start, running in all directions without ever grasping what was going on.* 'I had no idea of any of this.'

'There are two men who know the entire set-up. Flandin, who had no interest in a scandal erupting, and who's dead, and Bornand's head of security, Beauchamp. Beauchamp, a business associate of Chardon's – they were in Africa together in the seventies and every so often since then they've smuggled in a bit of Lebanese heroin. It was Beauchamp who met Cecchi at Mado's last weekend. And who was still with him when they met Bornand at the Perroquet Bleu. For the time being, that's all we know, but we're still digging. The papers found on Cecchi have been sent off for analysis. Beauchamp has been arrested. He's the lynchpin in the whole thing, that's certain. Who was he working for? A rival arms dealer? The Americans? The RPR which wanted to prevent the release of the hostages before the elections at all costs? All of the above? We may find out eventually. On the other hand, we can't count on an autopsy for Flandin. But that scarcely matters now.'

Fernandez's head's spinning. Macquart is triumphant.

'The fact that all that went over your head doesn't bother me. But the fact that you didn't talk to me about Chardon, that is serious. You were seen picking him up in Katryn's car the day of her murder. Fernandez, this memory lapse is one ruse too many. I warned you. You don't get a second chance.'

Fernandez is gutted. Macquart looks at his watch, 17.00 hours, time for the news. He switches on the transistor. News-flash on France Info.

'The Élysée press office has just informed us of the death of François Bornand, one of the President's closest friends and advisors. He was the victim of a hunting accident, at the home of his wife in the Saumur region. He was cleaning his shotgun without having checked whether it was loaded, when it went off, killing him outright. The President immediately sent his condolences to his widow. The funeral will take place tomorrow, in Saumur, in the strictest privacy.'

Macquart switches off the radio.

'You made the right choice in coming to see me, pity you didn't see things through to the end.'

Then with a wan and wholly ambiguous smile on his lips:

'The rule of law prevails. More or less.'

Afterword

In France, the 1980s were commonly referred to as the 'years of easy money', because during this decade money came to represent, for an entire political class and regardless of whether they were in power or in opposition, an end and a value in itself, at a time when entrepreneurs and financiers became the new heroes of modern times. The Socialists, who came to power with Mitterrand when he became President of the Republic in 1981 – having been sidelined over a period of decades – assumed and practised their new religion with the zeal of neophytes. Some among them exploited the situation to enrich themselves shamelessly. Making money, for these male politicians, took various forms as they sought to exercise influence in a number of different ways. One possible outlet was via the arms trade and there were serious pickings to be made, since after the Six Day War between Israel and the Arab countries in 1967, the Middle East has been in a state of constant upheaval.

In Lebanon, a massive influx of Palestinian refugees fighting for their national independence, primarily organised from within the heart of the Palestinian Liberation Organisation (PLO) succeeded in destabilising the already extremely fragile political and religious equilibrium of the country, torn apart by the civil war that lasted from 1975 to 1989. There were constant and confused armed conflicts between the Palestinians and the Lebanese militias, including the Shia (to whom Amal belonged); the Phalangists (right-wing Christians); and the

Druze (within the Progressive Socialist Party, or the PSP). Along with these internal conflicts in Lebanon, throughout the 1980s there hovered the permanent shadow of their more powerful neighbours. The shadow cast by Israel, seeking to eliminate all Palestinian resistance, and which invaded Lebanon twice over, bombing and laying siege to Beirut, occupied southern Lebanon for four years, that cast by Syria, with its dreams of annexation, which installed its army across a whole swathe of the country, and that of Iran, a Shia theocracy from 1979 onwards, manipulating religious influence as if it were a form of politics in order to emerge from isolation in an Islamic-Arab world heavily dominated by the Sunni.

At the other end of the Middle East, Shia Iran, where the Shah had been forced into exile by the Islamic Revolution of 1979, and Sunni Iraq (which supported the Palestinians in Lebanon), dedicated themselves to a conventional war which lasted from 1980–1988, a war of exceptional length and bloodshed, in which millions died. All these power games were in play during this decade, at the mercy of shifting allegiances, of terrorist acts of numerous kinds, involving the seizure of aeroplanes (even a cruise liner was boarded at sea), bombs and car bombs, mass murder, targeted assassinations, and – the latest change – suicide bombings, leaving thousands dead. Not to mention the taking of civilian hostages, to be used as negotiating tools.

France was deeply implicated in all these conflicts, and in more ways than one. Firstly, as is the way of French traditional politics in dealing with the Arab world, because it offered its support to Iraq by supplying it massively with arms, despite the official embargo. Then again, because of its wholesale adoption of a nuclear policy. The Shah of Iran was closely involved, ever since 1974, in the *Eurodif* uranium enrichment project. From 1979 onwards, France refused to honour the contractual accords made with Iran under the Ayatollahs. It therefore became the target of numerous attacks, instigated behind the scenes by Iran and involving the repeated seizure of – primarily – French and Lebanese hostages, of which the longest sequestration was that of Carton, Fontaine, Kauffman and Seurat, taken in March and May 1985, and which ended with three of them being released in May 1988, Seurat having died in captivity. The negotiations to obtain their release are central to this novel.

For the USA, this period was similarly extremely unsettled. The Iranians took the entire staff of the US Embassy in Tehran hostage, shortly after the fall of the Shah. Lengthy negotiations ensued, closely linked to Ronald Regan's victory at the presidential elections. Then a number of particularly bloody attacks led to the Americans' departure from Lebanon. Ultimately, Reagan became involved in the operation which came to be known as 'Irangate', and consisted of secretly selling arms to Iran (at that time under an official embargo) in order to release vast sums of black market money, then used to finance – outside any controls exercised by the US Congress – the 'Contras', ultra right-wing terrorist forces operating inside Nicaragua, in an attempt to destabilise the progressive regime then in power following the holding of the first ever democratic elections there.

It was a hugely eventful period offering almost unlimited opportunities and scope for wheeling and dealing. However, readers do not need to be familiar with every twist and turn to follow the plot, or at least that is my intention. Above all this novel is the story of men greedy for power and money. The sort of men one encounters, today as in bygone times, in Europe, the Middle East and the world over.

Dominique Manotti
November 2009

Notes

1. Philippe, Duke of Orleans, Regent of France, 1715–1723.
2. The heart of the Jewish district in Paris.
3. Société d'Électronique Appliquée (a fictitious company).
4. Banque Internationale du Liban/the International Bank of Lebanon (a fictitious bank).
5. GPRA/Gouvernement Provisionel de la Republique Algerienne: Bestégui is recounting to himself his first meeting with Bornand when he was still a young student, protesting against the war in Algeria and campaigning for self-determination, for broadly left-wing reasons. He remembers Bornand as a businessman who supported independence because the Americans did (being hostile to all forms of old colonialism that excluded them), and because the war was bad for business. Bornand, a war-time collaborator, is deeply hostile to de Gaulle.
6. The Organisation de l'armée secrète (OAS – or Organisation armée secrète, 'Secret Armed Organisation') was a short-lived, French far-right nationalist militant and underground organisation during the Algerian War (1954–62). The OAS used armed struggle in an attempt to prevent Algeria's independence.
7. EgyptAir Flight 648 was a Boeing 737 airliner hijacked in 1985 by the terrorist Abu Nidal Organisation. The subsequent raid on the aircraft by Egyptian troops led to dozens of deaths, making the hijacking one of the deadliest incidents in the history of aviation.